PLEASE, SIR

PLEASE, SIR

EROTIC STORIES OF FEMALE SUBMISSION

EDITED BY
RACHEL KRAMER BUSSEL

CLEIS
PRESS

Published in the United States by Cleis Press Inc., 2246 Sixth St., Berkeley, California 94710.

Printed in the United States.
Cover design: Scott Idleman
Cover photograph: Christine Kessler
Text design: Frank Wiedemann
Cleis Press logo art: Juana Alicia
First Edition.
10 9 8 7 6 5 4 3 2 1

ISBN: 978-1-57344-389-0

Contents

INTRODUCTION: RISK AND REWARD

If you ask me, submission is an art form. It requires dedication, focus, commitment and desire—and there's no single way of doing it. It's about unlocking something within yourself so you can reach beyond your normal limits, exposing your body and soul in order to go somewhere you cannot get to alone.

I had a lover who always told me that the key to life is "High risk, high reward." The same is true about kink, and this is evident throughout the stories in *Please, Sir*, which explores female submission and male dominance from the sub's point of view. When these characters take risks, they are rewarded...even when those rewards look like "punishment." They are rewarded in all kinds of ways, from being bound to being praised to being choked, spanked or put on display. They are rewarded by being tested again and again.

The women in these stories approach submission in different ways. Some, like Tess Danesi's protagonist in "I Breathe Your Name," live on the edge of fear and get off on pushing the limits

with their masters, though they don't always know where their
boldness will take them. Some of these women are drawn to
the charisma of a born leader, one like Krav Maga instructor,
Dominic, in Emerald's "Power over Power." Jackie, his student,
has been watching and fantasizing about him, but when he finally acknowledges her sexually, she is caught off guard:

> *I trembled, wanting to touch him but feeling frozen.*
> *Still looking at the ground, I nodded.*
> *With characteristic efficiency of motion, he*
> *reached with one finger and pulled my chin up. A*
> *shudder ran through me as I felt his power—the*
> *power I saw in every move he made, that he exuded*
> *at the front of the class, that he spoke when he told*
> *us what we were capable of, that coiled and expelled*
> *from him whenever he slammed any part of his body*
> *into the punching bag. This was the power that lived*
> *unquestioned within him, so seamlessly that it was*
> *as though it wouldn't exist without him.*

Others don't expect to be getting kinky at all, like the "Mommy's Boy" in Doug Harrison's story, where tables get turned
in a most delightful way. In Lisabet Sarai's "Stroke," a woman
risks getting kinky at work in order to realize her dream:

> *I just stood there, petrified by mingled fear and ex-*
> *citement. If anyone discovered us, I'd lose my job. I'd*
> *never work as a nurse again. Five years of education*
> *down the drain. But this might be my only chance.*
> *The chance to make my fantasies real.*

* * *

The lesson there, and in all of these stories, is that there is risk involved in submission. I don't mean the physical risks, but the emotional ones, the ones that require a leap of faith, a knowledge that what you are doing may unnerve you, confuse you and scare you, even while it makes you wet and eager and ready for more. As we see in Shanna Germain's opening story, "Anticipation," merely thinking about what he might do next, playing with power in one's own mind, can yield profound results:

> I can no longer breathe, much less make a noise of want. This is what he does to me, every day: whips me into a frenzy of words that makes me miss him more than I have the power to say, that makes me so wet that if he were here, I'd fuck him right now, bent over this table, with all these people watching, groaning his name with every thrust. I'd be begging him to fuck me, beat me, make me come with the kind of orgasm that makes everything else disappear.
>
> I have to go, back to the work that calls, the work that keeps me here in this foreign and fuckless place, but I don't want to.

Some, like Kissa Starling's heroine, are brats, and enjoy pushing their masters to the limit. Some don't deliberately provoke anyone but wind up bent over anyway. However they come to their submission (and come from their submission), their journey is one charged with the spark of passing power between two people, of welcoming the risk of submission and all it entails.

I like the women in this collection, and not just because they remind me of me when I'm reveling in being slapped across the face, forced to the ground, utterly at my chosen lover's (or master's, or partner's or top's) mercy. It's not just the actions here that are familiar, but the reasoning, the way they crave and cringe in the face of the power they are claiming, and the power they are giving up. They are smart enough to know that kink is not about simply embracing one's fears, but grappling with them, battling with them, taking risks and seeing if, in fact, they yield very sexy rewards.

Rachel Kramer Bussel
New York City

ANTICIPATION

Shanna Germain

I bought a bed, he says.

Actually, he doesn't say this. He types it. That's what the Instant Messenger window says while I wait for the rest of his thought: *Bard42 is typing.* I am sitting in a café in a small town in Germany, the only place I can get Internet. The Net is ridiculously priced, even here, but I don't care. It's the only thing I'm spending money on while I'm working my way across Europe. I cross my legs and stare at the screen of my laptop, a giant cup of coffee burning my palm.

I bought it mostly for the headboard, he types. *It has big, wide slats. Perfect for sliding a rope through. Or a belt. Or the pieces of your dress that I'm going to rip from your body.*

He is somewhere in the middle of New Hampshire, a place I've never been, a place I never wanted to go. He is somewhere in that state, in a new house, buying pieces of furniture. Buying them with me in mind. I can't even begin to tell him what this does to me.

I stood in the store and imagined you tied up against every headboard in the showroom. Walking from bed to bed, so stiff from the mere thought of you. This bed, with its strong, dark wood, was the one I saw your body against. Your pale wrists tied with my brown belt, legs spread-eagled so I can bury my face between those creamy thighs.

I close my eyes, savor this for as long as I can. I haven't seen him in almost six months. Some days, I can barely remember what he looks like. I have photos, of course, but they only capture his skin and bones. Not the essence of him, not the wicked mind or the way he looks at me over his wire-rims when he wants something from me. Not the bend of his fingers when he buries them in my long hair, forces me to my knees.

The men are delivering it tomorrow, he adds. *If you were here, I wouldn't even wait until they left before I bent you over the side of the mattress so that your ass was in the air, slid off my belt so they could hear the whistle, the sharp crack as it fell across your white curves. I'd let them hear every cry and moan you made.*

I have to bite back a quiet sound of want, swallow it down around my steaming coffee and hope that no one heard. It's bad enough to be the sole American in this small town, to know that I'm probably exuding the scent of my arousal, that I'm practically rocking in my seat with desire and want...to groan in public would be more than I can bear.

I think, the first time, I will make you wait, he types. *I will catch your wrists between the slats and rub the head of my cock between your legs until I'm coated in your heat, until you're soaked and begging. And then I will go and make dinner. I will cook steak and mushrooms, my cock hard, knowing the whole time that you're upstairs whimpering, aching, wanting.*

Now I do groan, the sound rising up accidentally before I

can bite it back, and I have to shift and cross my legs, the pulse of my clit beating hard inside my jeans. I'm not one of those women who can come just by rubbing their legs together, sadly. I need a hand on me, ideally his hand, hard and fast, spanking my ass or my clit, bringing me to that heated burn of orgasm. But I'll go back to my rented apartment and masturbate, thinking of him, his words, his brain. The myriad ways he comes up with to torture and please me.

What do you think? he types. *Sound like a decent plan for your arrival?*

I'm not as good with words as he is; he's the poet after all. The wordsmith. I am all business and science. I mostly type things like, *It sounds ideal. I miss the sound of your belt sliding through your belt loops. I wish you were folding your hands around my wrists, holding me down while I come.* Stupid things like that. He doesn't seem to mind. I think, for him, my reaction is enough. Knowing he makes me wet and aching while I'm sitting in a public place. The way my face turns pink when I'm horny or embarrassed.

This time I answer his question with a simple, *Yes, please.* And the refrain sings in my head. Yes, please. How often I've said that for him, to him. Harder? Yes, please. Tighter? Yes, please. More? Yes, yes, please.

Good girl, he types, and I can almost hear the growl in it. The guttural broken sound his voice takes on when he's fucking me, and he's right on the verge of coming, trying to keep in charge of himself. The one time I can take control if I want it, pushing him over the edge with a slide of my hips or the cry of his name.

*My only worry...*he types. And then he stops. He does this when we're fucking, too. He'll tie me to a railing or a chair, loops and loops of rope holding me still and open for him, entirely exposed, and he'll slide a blindfold across my eyes and say, "You know what I'm going to do to you now?" and then he doesn't answer, doesn't finish. Just lets me whip myself into a frenzy of fear and want, straining to hear every sound. Is that the jingle of a belt buckle or a dog collar? The click of a knife opening or a door shutting? He waits until I am shuddering with want and anticipation and then finally, finally, he'll answer.

What? I practically beg. *What?*

If I was there right now, I know I'd be hearing his laughter. His real laugh, not the one he puts on for show. The one that's just for me, that dark-edged sound of wicked mirth that I miss almost as much as his sadistic sense of fucking.

Well, as long as it's been since I've fucked you, he types, *it's going to be hard. Cruel. I'm going to tie you tight and drive you so hard against the headboard that you won't be able to breathe, every stroke burying my cock in your body. Your throat, your cunt, your asshole. I bought a paddle today and a gorgeous glass dildo. I'm going to use them both, at once. Fill you and spank you and fuck you. Until your skin is red and marred, until you're bent and breathless and broken...*

I just hope the headboard can take it.

Oh, fuck. I can no longer breathe, much less make a noise of want. This is what he does to me, every day: whips me into a frenzy of words that makes me miss him more than I have the power to say, that makes me so wet that if he were here, I'd fuck him right now, bent over this table, with all these people watching, groaning his name with every thrust. I'd be begging him to fuck me, beat me, make me come with the kind of orgasm that makes everything else disappear.

I have to go, back to the work that calls, the work that keeps me here in this foreign and fuckless place, but I don't want to.

Two more months, I type. Two more months and then I will

be allowed to go home, to our new house, the one that he's decorating with me—with fucking me—in mind.

Two more months, he agrees. *I'm planning on it.*

I have to go, I type. And there is so much ache and want buried in the cold, hard words. I hope he can hear it. Somehow, I think he can.

The IM tells me, *Bard42 is typing,* and so I wait before I sign off, the heat of my arousal pulsing hard between my thighs, sending up the sweet scent of desire as I move in the chair. I know that if I buried my fingers into the center of me right now, I'd be slick and slippery, lubed by want.

Next week, he types, *I'm going to buy a coffee table. Something sturdy and strong, just the right size to lay you down on your stomach, and tie your wrists and ankles to the legs. And then I'm going to whip you, baby, until your ass is hot pink and marred, until your cunt opens for me like the palest flower, until you're begging me to stop. Because we both know I never will.*

The IM tells me *Bard42 has signed off,* and I follow suit. *Two months,* I think as I close my laptop with a click and a sigh. Two months and then I can be whole again: Captured by more than words. Tied up by more than want. Beaten by things other than schedules and time.

I'm planning on it.

BECAUSE HE CAN

Elizabeth Coldwell

I suppose, deep down, I must want my husband to find out about Adam, because I'm usually so good at keeping secrets. Tell me something in confidence and that's where it stays, even though at least one close friend of mine risks losing her marriage and another her job if ever I let slip what they carelessly asked me to keep secret after one too many glasses of chardonnay. So in neglecting to close the email I've been composing when I hear David's voice calling up the stairs, letting me know he's home, I must be sending him some kind of message. Or maybe a challenge. David loves it when I challenge his authority.

We suit each other so well in that regard. He often refers to me as his little minx, deliberately provocative and thoroughly disrespectful. He understands my need to be disciplined, to be made to follow his instructions or give him pleasure when he demands it. He can get me wet simply with a look or by altering the tone of his voice. He is strict but loving, and I worship him above everything.

Adam, of course, knows nothing of this. I may have been flirting shamelessly with him since the day he joined our department, but it's all been completely vanilla. We swap dirty emails in quiet moments, but though I might tell him I want to be fucked from behind, I don't mention that it's while I'm wearing a blindfold and restraints. And he has absolutely no idea about those fantasies I have where he's ordered me onto my knees to suck his cock, with our office door closed but not locked, and the boss's secretary likely to burst in at any moment. I don't intend to explain my need to submit, because this is strictly a virtual relationship, just a way of spicing up a boring day at work, and destined to remain so—until I forget about that email.

I'm in the kitchen, washing the dishes after dinner—a chore David often likes to watch me perform while I'm dressed in nothing but a silly, frilly apron, though tonight I'm wearing a more practical combination of oversized T-shirt and yoga pants—when I hear him come up behind me. He wraps his arms around me, his big body enveloping mine. His lips gently nuzzle my neck and I'm relaxing into his embrace, when he murmurs, "So, tell me about Adam."

It may seem like a strange question to ask out of the blue, but we often discuss work and the friends we have made there with each other, so I don't think too much of it. "I'm sure I've told you about him before," I reply. "He's been with the company about eighteen months, he joined the department just before Christmas from the Birmingham branch and I think he has a flat over in that new development on the riverside."

"Fascinating," David says, "but none of that explains quite why you want to lick his cock like it's the sweetest lollipop you've ever tasted."

That's when I realize he's read the email. From David's lips, those words sound so cloying and predictable, but that's the kind of language I use with Adam. It's the language he under-stands.

My husband always knows when I'm lying, so I don't even try to evade the question. I turn around and gaze up into his dark, wise eyes. "Because he's cute," I say. "And I like to have messages like that waiting for him when he gets to the office in the morning, because I know that when I arrive, he'll already be hard just thinking about what I said."

"Really?" David quirks an eyebrow. "Sounds like my little minx fancies herself as some kind of expert in control games now. You're not trying to top this cute friend of yours on the quiet, are you?"

"Not at all," I assure him. "I don't think he'd even know what a top was if you asked him."

"Well, why don't I? Ask him, I mean." David must see the look of horror that crosses my face, because he says, "Let's go to bed and talk about this." That's when I begin to suspect where this is heading, because all the big, important conversations we have about sex and our relationship take place in bed.

I let David lead me up the stairs to the bedroom and lie back on the bed to watch as he quickly strips naked. His cock is al-ready beginning to swell and harden, and I want to grab it and play with it, but he won't allow me that privilege just yet. First, I must hear out whatever plan has been forming in his mind since he saw the message I was writing to Adam.

He joins me on the bed and peels the T-shirt off over my head, then pushes me back on the bedcovers and grasps both my wrists above my head with one of his big, strong hands—a simple, but powerful demonstration of his mastery over me. I lie there quietly, wondering what he's about to say.

"Nicky, you remember how we once talked about what we would do if we were ever really, seriously attracted to another person, and whether we should act on that attraction?"

"Yes," I reply, as I feel his free hand stroking softly over the curve of my bare breast. "We said that each of us would be allowed a little adventure, as long as we were completely honest about it."

"Well, I'm assuming you haven't had an adventure as yet, because you haven't exactly been honest about your naughty love notes to Adam, have you?"

I want to protest. I haven't said anything because there has been nothing to tell David about. But then I've just confessed to sending Adam messages which were expressly designed to get him hard, and so I have to concede that my husband might just have a point.

Suddenly, David's gentle caress becomes a tight pinch of my nipple. He uses just enough pressure to send sparks of sensation racing down to my pussy, and I gasp in a mixture of pain and arousal. His voice drops, becomes more of a growl, rich with authority. I know that tone so well, and I writhe against the covers. "I'm giving you permission to have that adventure, Nicky, but on the condition that you let Adam know what you're really like. He obviously has no idea what a filthy-minded, kinky little minx you are, and so we're going to show him. You invite Adam to the house, and I'll give him a demonstration of the best way to treat you. If he can cope with that, he's all yours. If he can't—well, is it really worth your while bothering with him?"

I can't quite believe what my husband is suggesting. My submission to him has always been our private little secret; we have no friends who share our lifestyle and we never go out to play on the club scene. Now here he is telling me he's going to dominate me in front of someone else—someone who he will allow to dominate me, too, if he proves himself up to the task. For a

moment, I wonder why David is proposing this. And then I realize: it's because he can.

It proves surprisingly easy to persuade Adam to come over for
dinner. From the hints I drop, he gains the impression that David and I are interested in a threesome, though naturally I don't
fill him in on the finer points. That will be David's task, at the
appropriate moment. It's clearly a thrill for him to be offered
the chance of sex with an older, more experienced couple, and I
suspect that he won't be able to resist sharing the details afterward. "This is nothing to brag about to your friends," I warn
him. "Not if you want to be invited back."

At seven the following Saturday night, there's a knock on
the door. I'm putting the final touches to the table settings, and
David is relaxing in the lounge with a beer. Music is playing on
the CD system, some Ibiza chill-out album that David is particularly fond of. Adam is on the doorstep, clutching a bottle
of champagne. He smells of musky aftershave and nervous anticipation as I take the proffered bottle from him and usher him
inside. If he's surprised to see that I'm wearing a Chinese pat-
terned silk robe rather than anything more formal, he tries not
to let it show. He'll be far more surprised in a moment.

My husband rises from his chair to shake Adam's hand.
"Nice to meet you, mate." As they share a manly embrace, I decide that no one could ever accuse me of going for a type. David
is close to six foot, with a nose broken in a couple of places from
his years as an amateur boxer and the first traces of gray appearing in his black hair. Adam, by contrast, is boyishly blond and
only a little taller than I am. If I were simply going to be fucked
by both of them, it would be a more than enticing prospect. But
throw a little domination play into the mixture, and I'm already
beginning to feel my pussy pulsing with excitement.

"Before we go any further," David says to Adam, "I need to tell you what's going to happen tonight. Yeah, I know Nicky probably made you think this was just a simple three in a bed setup, but there's a lot more to it than that. You see, I'm offering you the chance to spend lots of quality time with my wife, but only if you're prepared to treat her the way she likes to be treated. Nicky, display yourself."

It's a command he's given me many times before, but never when someone else has been present. I don't hesitate to do as he asks, though. I want my husband to be proud of me, and I want my potential lover to see how obedient and well trained I am. I unfasten the tie of the robe and let the garment drop from my shoulders. Naked, I sink to my knees, legs slightly parted, palms on my thighs. Gazing straight ahead, I wait for my next instruction.

Adam is staring at me. He seems slightly stunned, which is understandable, given that he's just watched me strip off and get into a position which is designed to draw attention to my most intimate places simply because my husband told me to, but the look he's giving me suggests he likes what he sees.

"Would you like a beer, mate?" David asks. When Adam nods, David snaps, "Nicky, get your friend a beer."

I hurry into the kitchen, and take out one of the bottles of beer which have been chilling in the fridge. When I return to the lounge, David and Adam are both sitting in armchairs, discussing the afternoon's football results as though this is a perfectly ordinary social gathering.

When I hand the beer to Adam, I'm aware that he can't drag his attention from my breasts. "I know this looks weird," David says, "but trust me, Nicky is enjoying this. We both are. She likes to be dominated, and I like to dominate her. I tell her what to do and she obeys, and we get off on it. I spank her bottom from time to time, and she absolutely loves that. But I think you need more of a demonstration to convince you, don't you?"

David invites Adam to join him at the table. It takes Adam a moment to realize that there are only two place settings. The reason for this quickly becomes apparent as I begin to serve the meal. It's a simple collection of cold cuts, designed to be eaten mostly with the fingers. When the two men have helped themselves to generous amounts of rare roast beef, ham and salad, David chooses some tidbits for a third plate. Without even being told, I go to sit on the floor at the side of his chair. As he and Adam eat, they continue to discuss sport and television programs and music, finding out just how much they have in common. At no point am I included in the conversation. Every so often, David will feed me a piece of chicken or tomato, or give me a sip of wine from the glass he's poured for me, treating me like a favored pet. Though he's acting as though I'm not there, he is, in fact, completely aware of my needs, maintaining the subtle balance between the controller and the controlled.

Adam, of course, is finding it much harder to be so nonchalant, and David is aware of this. He ruffles my hair affectionately and says, "Nicky, crawl under the table for me. I want you to find out how much Adam is enjoying this."

I push my way under the hem of the tablecloth and crawl on hands and knees to where Adam is sitting. Slowly, I run my fingers up his jeans-clad leg, coming to rest on the sizeable lump in his crotch. "Oh, he's hard," I murmur approvingly.

"Take it out, then," David orders. "Take it out and suck it."

I fumble with the buttons of his fly, reaching in to where his cock is beginning to uncoil and fetching it out into the open. My fingers close around him, fingertips barely touching. It's been a long time since I've played with any man other than David, and I take a moment to savor the way Adam looks—long, smooth shaft and neat head sheathed in a sleeve of velvety skin—and breathe in his distinctly salty scent. Above me, slightly muffled by the thick linen tablecloth, I can hear the two men still carrying on their conversation, though Adam's voice is beginning to crack in places, and when my lips close round his cockhead, he loses the power of speech entirely.

"How is that?" David enquires casually as I start to suck.

"Good," Adam stammers.

That's not answer enough for David, who presses him. "Enough suction? Too much in the way of teeth? You can tell her, you know. Whatever you want, she'll do it."

I should be offended by the offhand way in which my husband is critiquing my oral technique, but I'm not. Everything he says is true. Whatever he—or Adam—wants, I will do. For me, that's the turn-on: being made to take orders, and taking pride in completing them to the best of my ability. I am determined to give Adam a blow job he'll never forget, to please him—and to please David.

"Suck harder, Nicky," Adam demands, a new, stronger edge to his voice. "And take me deeper down your throat." There's no talk of sweet lollipops now, nor any sign of all the light-hearted teasing that characterized our email flirtation, and I'm beginning to wonder whether I've underestimated him. Even faced with such a willingly submissive woman as myself, some men wouldn't have been able to cope with this situation, but not Adam. The way he's ordering me around suggests he's either a very fast learner or he has a dominant streak lurking just under the surface.

As I continue to lavish the best of my attention on his cock, gripping the base in my fist and bobbing my head down onto his length, I feel the tablecloth being lifted off my body. David is baring my backside, which is thrust out toward him. His fingers probe my pussy gently, and I don't need to hear his little chuckle of approval to know that he's discovered just how wet I am.

"You're loving this, aren't you, minx?" David says, but my mouth is too full of Adam's cock for me to speak. By way of answer, I thrust my bum back onto his hand. One of his fingers, thickly coated with my own juices, toys with the entrance to my arse for a moment before slipping inside with almost embarrassing ease. Another finger starts to rub my clit, and I know he wants me to lose control before Adam can come in my mouth. The willful part of me is determined not to let that happen, and I suck even harder, using all the little tricks I know to bring Adam to the point where he can't hold back any longer.

Adam reaches down under the table, letting his fingers tangle in my long curls and holding my head firmly in place as his seed shoots down my throat. Finally, he releases his grip and sighs, "That was amazing," but I can barely hear him, because David presses just that little bit deeper inside me and I can't fight him any longer. My muscles clench around his finger and I'm coming, almost sobbing with pleasure and gratitude to my husband for making this wonderful moment happen. I fall forward into Adam's lap, his slowly subsiding erection pressing against my cheek.

"You can come out now," David tells me, and I crawl out on slightly shaky limbs. He scoops me up into his embrace. I'm acutely aware that he's the only one of our little trio who's yet to receive any satisfaction, but I'm sure it won't be too long before I'm required to put that right.

"So, Adam," David says, "do you think you can treat my little minx here the way she needs to be treated?"

Adam nods and smiles, and I know I'm about to learn what it really means to submit to two such very different men. I can't believe how much I'm looking forward to it.

So it seems as though David and I have both got what we really wanted, I think, as I go to the kitchen, still proudly naked, to make coffee for the three of us. He set me this challenge because he could, and I responded to it so enthusiastically because I could. Next week, I'll start sending Adam emails where I share all those fantasies I've hidden from him till now, and perhaps the next time I go down on my knees to suck him, it will be under his desk, with the boss's secretary just the other side of our unlocked office door.

AVERY SAYS

Sommer Marsden

It's at the party that I can't quite still my tongue. I really can't. I see my openings and I jump. I pounce. I push my boundaries and poke the bear, as my mother used to say.

"They say the average person gains a pound a year," Thomas says and I try to bite my tongue, I really do. I literally bite it, pinching the traitorous muscles between my strong white teeth.

I say it anyway. "You've always been an overachiever, honey," I say, and pat the very small protrusion of his belly. In ten years he may have gained five pounds. He is by no means heavy. He does not deserve my scathing remark. And yet, I say it. And to make matters worse, I stroke his belly as if he were the Buddha.

My Aunt Ann starts. My Aunt Mary blushes, drops her gaze, backs away as if my cruelty is contagious. Thomas frowns, frowns and flushes with deserved anger, but he does not raise his voice. Does not remove my stroking hand from his dark blue shirt, or even embarrass me back. He does not imply that I am not the size eight I once was. Or that my breasts do not point due north as they did once upon a time. He does not mention the tiny streaks of silver in my blonde hair. He smiles at me.

He *smiles* at me.

And fear whips up my spine like a downed live wire. Thrashing and spreading sparks of panic worry along my skin. But my cunt jumps to life, going warm and tight and wet for that smile. Because that smile means I am in big trouble. Big trouble means pain. But big trouble also means pleasure. My nipples peak and I try to hide my shiver from the aunts.

"I'll get you more wine," my husband says softly and walks into the Christmas crowd.

I bite my lip and straighten my dress, tug at my earrings, fix my stockings. All to fend off the thumping excitement and sexual arousal that washes over me. I feel lightheaded and hot, scared and excited. I honestly feel like I might come right there in my mother's dining room in the soft glow of white Christmas lights under the sharp and critical gaze of distant relatives. The thought alone nearly trips me into orgasm.

"So how are the boys?" I ask my aunts and watch the clock while they give an answer I do not hear.

Thomas makes me wait one hour and fifty-one minutes before he leans in and says into my ear, "Get your nasty little ass in the car in the next five minutes or it will be ten times worse than whatever you are imagining." Under the guise of hugging me to him, he pulls me in and pinches my right asscheek so hard that tears spring to my eyes and I choke on the air in my lungs. I nod so he knows that I understand and I say my hurried good-byes with a mixture of dread and anticipation twisting in my belly.

In the car, he says not a word. He lifts the skirt of my black dress, and checks. I am in the thigh-high hose and garters. I have on a small silken pair of black panties. He puts a finger inside the crotch and touches me just long enough to test me, to see how wet I am. He does not touch me to give me pleasure but to gauge my readiness, the way a mechanic would check the oil in a car: Detached. Professional. All business. I jump under his touch anyway, stealing as much pleasure from his fingertip as I possibly can.

"You know we start off with fifteen. Don't give me a reason to up it, Avery. My hand won't be light tonight. What you did doesn't even deserve comment. You know that."

I nod and now the tears are coming. What have I done? Why did I do it? What was I thinking? But under it all is the thumping in my cunt from where he has just touched me and the crawling anxiety that somehow makes it all feel so much better—more intense, sharper and brighter and more real.

"I know."

We drive home in silence.

I shift in my seat, crossing and uncrossing my legs as the heater blows hot air across my knees. "Sit still," he commands. So I do.

In the driveway, he turns all the knobs, fiddles with the glove compartment. He is making me wait and my throat feels small and the air feels thick. "Get on the porch, Avery." His voice is soft but full of menace. I exit the car and make my way up onto our porch. A small square of concrete framed with black wrought-iron fence. Two small chairs and a bistro table grace the porch. Above my head, our porch light glows, spotlighting me in the dark December night.

Thomas is examining his keys as he comes up the walk. I clench my thighs together and that only makes the pressure in my pussy worse. My want is worse. My fear is worse. I feel like I'm spiraling and I try to breathe deeply. I can't. His loafers whisper secretively on the steps and he looks up at me, big brown eyes soft with love. His voice is hard with discipline when he sits on a chair and says, "Over my knees, Avery."

I gulp air. Here? Outside? In the open? On the porch? It is late but not *that* late. This time of night at this time of year lots of people could be awake: young parents playing Santa, lonely people with insomnia, the older couple who stay up late to eat popcorn and watch Christmas movies. I inhale. He is joking. Surely he is joking.

My husband looks up, smiles. His eyes are so kind. "Now. Right this moment. Or I'll make it twenty and we'll do it in the middle of the street under a streetlight." He pats his lap and I drop to my knees without thinking. The concrete rips at my fragile stockings and I know they have torn, torn at the knees like a whore's. I drape myself over his lap. The light and the word *whore* in my head and the circumstances have my cunt nearly dripping and a shameful blush heats my cheeks. My breath plumes out before me, a cold white ghost as he lifts my skirt and palms my ass with a gentle care that is staggering.

My husband begins his spanking. He is humming "Deck the Halls" as he delivers the first seven blows. I squirm and I kick. The pain is frightening and lovely. My cunt is clutching around nothing and my hosiery is further shredding as my knees scrape and bleed.

"You'd better stay still. Your knees will be in ribbons before I'm done." And then he hisses, *eight.* "Eighth spank for the girl with the nasty tongue. Avery says things she shouldn't. Avery says things to shock..." He pauses and the blows come harder, faster. Heat sears my skin and my pussy flickers, dances, begs. *Fuck me, fuck me, fuck me,* is the chant in my head.

"I'm sorry," is what comes out of my mouth.

"Shut up. I don't want to know what Avery has to say right now. Twelve should be wonderfully excruciating," he says, and he hits me right at the seam of my ass, the sensitive bundle of nerves that divides left cheek from right. My head flies back and I let out a howl. I see a light wink off in the neighbor's house. I know he is watching. My neighbor, Mr. Berger: he can see me. He is a widower. He is watching. The thirteenth blow washes that thought from my mind.

When Thomas worms his fingers into my panties and pushes them into me brutally hard, the thought returns. He will see. He will see. They will see. Everyone will see me, punished, on my knees, bleeding, squirming, begging, coming. God, he will see me coming. And Thomas is with me, right there. The fourteenth and fifteenth blows land a bit harder but slower and his fingers push right in the perfect place, right against that swollen sweet spot deep inside of me. I throw my head back as I come, bare my face to the dark and blank window next door. I see him in my mind, Mr. Berger, see him watching me, touching his cock, jerking off as Thomas shows the world how bad I am but how well I take my punishment, how sweetly I can come.

My ass is on fire, my hair trailing the cracked concrete porch. Thomas takes his fingers from me as I nuzzle his hard-on through his gray dress slacks. I push my pelvis at his leg, humping against him, showing him I don't want to be done.

"I'm taking you inside. You bad girl. You dirty whore. And then what? What will you do? What do whores do?" His voice is just loud enough to carry if someone should be listening.

"I'll get on my knees," I say on a breath.

"You'll get on your knees. Your bloody busted knees and…"

"I'll suck your cock. Please, Thomas, let me." My voice is just loud enough to float to eavesdropping ears.

He is unlocking the door and I do not bother to smooth my dress over my blazing ass or fix my panties that are hiked to the side. My knees sting with a delicious pain. My body is in perfect chaos. We're barely inside when I drop to my knees. They sing with agony but I smile. I open my mouth and then Thomas is fucking my face, sliding between my lips, pulling my hair.

"Avery says the nastiest things," he says as he comes. I use my tongue for something besides caustic remarks. I lick at him until he makes me stop.

There will be more, I know. He will fuck me, clean me, tend my bruises. Love me. Until the next time I open my mouth and the wrong thing comes out. And then he will punish me.

THE SUB FAIRY

Mercy Loomis

Guests meandered in and out of the room, the air filled with the babble of a dozen different conversations. She-Ra joked loudly with a guy in a white lab coat. A flapper who had relinquished her cigarette holder in favor of a cup of punch sat with crossed legs on the knee of Darth Maul. My husband Sean, dressed all in black as usual, but with a cape and tunic over his poet shirt, was talking computers with a man dressed as his own evil twin. Sean leaned forward in the chair, gesturing with one hand, and the other man nodded thoughtfully.

I sat quietly on the floor at Sean's feet, pretending to listen to what he was saying. It was a prosaic scene, Halloween costumes aside, a full house of thirtysomethings, eating, drinking, and talking politics.

It was not a situation in which I normally found myself quivering with arousal.

My costume was a gothic dream, a sort of wingless twilight fairy, clad in a shimmering uneven dark blue skirt over floor-length black, a silky off-the-shoulder black blouse, and a dark blue and silver corset to tie it all together. A silver half-mask hid my face, though it showed enough that I had to continuously school my expression.

Sean's other hand was hidden under the black lace veil that was attached to my mask and flowed down my back to my waist. His hand lay heavy and possessive against the back of my neck, his fingers occasionally tugging at the choker I wore, or sliding up to wind themselves in my hair, pulling my head back against his knee.

Right there, in the middle of a crowded room, we were having foreplay. And no one knew.

I *loved* it.

I had never consciously wanted more, sexually, than I already had. After years of happy marriage, with never a complaint about our bedroom activities, I had felt more than blessed. Sure, bondage and domination in books or movies got me hot, but I'd never thought I wanted to actually experience them.

And yet, as we made love I would so often have that imagery in my mind: restraints, ropes, blindfolds; the idea of being held down, taken, and enjoying every second of it.

I don't know what gave me the courage to say it (I've always been shy when it comes to pillow talk), but I do remember what put it in my head. A book, "housewife porn" as Sean would say, a romance full of all the wonderful BDSM things that had been making merry in my imagination.

The idea of having to ask permission to come wasn't new, and I don't know why it stuck with me that time. But about a week after I finished the book, as Sean was teasing my clit and the tremors were beginning to run through me, I forced the words out.

"Can I come?"

There was a pause before he said, "Yes," and I might've thought that I had freaked him out, if the energy level in the room hadn't jumped like a frog on a griddle. Still, we didn't really discuss it afterward.

But I had liked it—quite a bit. And I thought he did, too.

So I tried again.

It wasn't planned. We were lying in bed, and I had asked, as I often do, "So what would you like?" By that I meant, as long as I get an orgasm out of it, I'm up for pretty much anything. He had rolled onto his back, saying, "How about you suck me?" And I knelt next to him on the bed, my head and eyes lowered, and said quietly, "You could *tell* me to."

It was easier this time, which was strange to me, since "Can I come?" is sort of a heat of the moment kind of thing, and this was much more blatant, almost confrontational. But I felt that same excitement in the air, and when I glanced sidelong at his face, all I saw was lust and eagerness.

In that same calm, confident way he talks to animals and clients, he said, "Suck me."

Did I ever.

I'm gifted with a definite oral fixation and a husband who loves to be teased. That night I spent a full hour lavishing attention on his cock, working hard to maintain the mindset that I was there to fulfill his needs, to serve him, and not to just go until I got a little tired. I started slow, with light kisses that grew more intense, adding flicks of my tongue along the shaft. I breathed over the skin of his sac, caressing it with my fingers, my lips, my tongue. Then I moved back to his cock, running up the whole length in a wet line so I could nibble, gently, at the edge of his head, mouth burrowing into that border zone, sucking at the skin. I took the full length of him in one quick thrust of my head, just to feel his body clench, and went back to my slow torment.

The orgasm took him hard, at the end, with my mouth all around him, rubbing him against my hard palate with every suck. I squeezed his balls and worked him with my tongue, listening with pleased satisfaction to the volume of his cries. And when the shudders stopped and he began to soften, I slipped off to the bathroom to spit and rinse, and came sauntering back with a feeling not only of pride, but also of unmistakable afterglow.

I knew I had pleased him, and that knowledge left me sated and content.

We talked quite a bit after that night.

Now, three months later, I was parked at his feet in a sort of passive-aggressive display of submission. There was a dearth of seating, it was true, and my corset forced me to sit up straight, but I felt as though I were holding a sign that read, *That's my dom. Mine. Mine, mine, mine.*

Tonight, in my fairy-tale outfit, I knew I was beautiful. The mask that hid my features but displayed my tiny smile made me mysterious. The corset emphasized my curves, the low neckline of the blouse revealing my generous cleavage for all and sundry. My curled legs were hidden in the fabric of my skirts, my hands in their black opera gloves relaxed, unmoving in my lap. I held my shoulders proudly, rolled back and down to emphasize the graceful arch of my neck; the demure tilt of my head and subtle twist in my posture announcing to anyone, or so I felt, that Sean and Sean alone held my undivided attention.

I imagined how I must look, and was pleased with the effect. *Maybe a little silver chain,* I mused, *something delicate, attached to my choker. I could be a captive fairy, after all.*

The idea of making myself little more than an ornament for his costume, a living accessory, got me frighteningly wet. I didn't understand the appeal, I truly didn't, but after months of muttering, "I don't know why I like this, but I do," I accepted it without question. I visualized that lovely silver leash and quivered, hot and aching, until it was time to go home.

Following him out to the car, I settled myself carefully in the passenger seat. As Sean pulled out of the driveway, I reached up to take off my mask, but he stopped me.

"Leave it," he said. His voice had that husky, steely ring that said he wasn't done topping me yet. "Put your seat back."

I did, arranging my veil on my right shoulder so it wouldn't obstruct the view. He reached over, slid his hand down my shirt.

"Open your legs."

I spread them as much as I could, my right foot up on the dash, left knee bent, my skirt pulled high. The long material draped my legs, even with the fabric drawn all the way up on one side, hiding his hand as he transferred his attention from my breast to my clit. I wasn't wearing any panties. He'd told me not to.

"That's a wet little toy," he purred to me as we drove down the highway. "Did you like sitting there all nice and submissive?"

His dexterous fingers were stroking me, dipping inside me, then circling my clit, dipping and circling, over and over again. "Oh, yes," I moaned. I was already beginning to shake.

"You going to come nice and loud for me?"

It was only a question because he liked to hear me answer him. "Yes!"

"Good." And he lightened his touch, that bastard, keeping me on the brink, bringing me so close and then backing off with a "Not yet," all the way through town, lingering at stop signs, stopping for every yellow light, while I burned under his fingers and the imaginary eyes of every car we passed, until five blocks from home he finally said, "Come for me."

I was still shrieking when he pulled into the driveway.

Tomorrow we would get up and mow the lawn, do laundry, clean the house, and all the other stuff that happens on a weekend. We might go grocery shopping, or out to a movie, or any of the other things we had always done before.

But in the back of our minds was the knowledge that, at any time, he could grab me and throw me over the couch, or tell me to get down on my knees, and I would do it, happily.

Marriage just doesn't get any better than this.

I BREATHE YOUR NAME

Tess Danesi

It's the feeling of absence that wakes me. Normally, when I first stir, Dar's hard chest is pressed to my back, his exhalations soft and warm on my shoulder, his arm draped weightily over my chest. His presence is a heavy one, ominous at times and comforting at others. Whether it's because of his size—at six three he looks down on most of us mere mortals—or the gravitas that often defines his state of mind, I'm used to feeling surrounded, even encompassed by him. Regardless, it's a feeling I treasure.

As I slowly rouse, stretching my arms over my head, feeling the weight of my heavy breasts, dusky nipples erect in the air-conditioning, shifting upward, I recall him, what must have been hours ago, whispering in my ear, "Come run with me this morning, pet." Glancing at the clock on the bedside table, I see it is now just seven in the morning. I don't clearly recall answering him. I love my sleep and tend to rise slowly. And it's a weekend; I don't have to be up. Dar, however, rarely varies his routines. So, given that it would have been about five, I'm sure I just turned over, groaned unintelligibly and was instantly slumbering peacefully again, leaving him to run by himself. This is as it should be. At five foot two, my pace is not very speedy at all, and Dar runs as if to punish himself. I much prefer the slow stretch of a yoga class to pounding the pavement. When I want to punish myself, I have only to goad Dar and I can be assured he'll do so in ways that fulfill me on a much deeper level.

Sitting up, I brush back several long mahogany strands of hair that have decided to adhere stubbornly to my bottom lip and then let my toes dig deep into the thick-piled antique Persian rug, a rug softened by strands of silks woven painstakingly into the complex design. Dar, while requiring little, is fond of excellence and craftsmanship in his creature comforts. His hard-earned money gives him the means to indulge most of those excesses. With me, he has the means to indulge his more sadistic excesses.

Despite it being mid-July, the air-conditioning makes me shudder now that I have emerged from my cocoon of blankets. Stroking my palms along my arms to ward off the chill, I find myself closing my eyes, enjoying the eroticism of skin on soft, creamy skin. Before long, my mind has begun to transpose my light touch with Dar's rough one. Evidence of his sadism, my own masochism really, is often written clearly on my body, necessitating carefully chosen clothing on most workdays. I love each of the bruises that linger for weeks on my skin. Pressing them, feeling the dull ache, brings the memory of his touch back to me, but I realize that others will more than likely see them in a very different light. Rising, I wrap myself in the light cotton robe that rests over the arm of the club chair.

As I near the bathroom, I hear the sound of the shower and close my eyes for a moment, picturing Dar, soaked black hair just long enough to caress his collar clinging to his head and dripping down the back of his neck, water droplets beading on his smooth olive skin. I feel a familiar, pleasurable tension shift to my cunt at the thought. My clit throbs as I recall other scenes that have taken place in his sleekly modern bathroom. The time he came upon me showering, breaking his number-one rule—make sure to turn on the ventilation fan when you shower. As punishment, he turned the ecstasy of my shower into a trial of endurance by simply changing the temperature from blissfully warm to freezing cold. But, as usual with Dar, pleasure follows pain. That I have chosen to endure the pain, or even find pleasure in it, confuses my best friend, Maggie. Hell, just what motivates my quest for pleasure through suffering confounds me at times. But then, Dar had wrapped my shivering body in a large fluffy towel and carried me to bed. With his warm body pressed to mine, my teeth stopped chattering and my body stopped shaking. I stopped questioning and just surrendered to one sensation after another. Finally, he turned me onto my belly, raised my hips high and plunged into my depths, each increasingly brutal thrust of his hot, hard cock melting away my lingering icy anger until the harshness I had endured only minutes before seemed light-years away. That's Dar's magic. Like wind taking the billowy smoke rising from a chimney, Dar's kiss, his touch, his words of endearment and declarations of love disperse the suffering I've endured.

I realize how this sounds, I do. You're probably thinking, *Oh, poor deluded thing, she's being abused and doesn't even know it.* But I assure you, this is not the case. I went into my relationship with Dar over two years ago with eyes wide open to the level of his sadism. He never lied about his dark desires; if anything, he made himself out to be far worse than the reality. And I craved it then as I still do now. While no one has ever been capable of causing me pain in the way that Dar does, neither has anyone ever been so tirelessly my champion. I am his to cherish and to protect and to hurt, but not harm, as he sees fit.

There have been times he's gone too far, times when he has left my faith in him shattered into so many jagged little shards that neither of us were sure we could repair the damage. Through him, I've found that my own heart isn't always as light and loving as I like to think it is. In this very bathroom, the threshold of which I am about to cross, I sat with briny tears burning undulating trails down my cheeks contemplating how, for once, I could make him suffer. I settled on holding the straight razor that has been his shaving preference for years to his throat while he slept. Not to cut him. No, not that. But to see his eyes open wide in fear, to see his cool, always-in-control demeanor crumble, in the misguided hope that he'd understand all that I have endured for him. Had I been thinking clearly, that it wouldn't end well, or at least not with my desired outcome, would have been obvious from the start. But we managed to come through even that. I can't say that he fears me now; we both know the truth is that the only danger he was in that night was of the razor accidentally falling from my trembling hand.

Now, all I want to do is watch the man I love shower, an act that never fails to arouse me beyond all comprehension, and when he's done, to make him forgo a towel altogether and to dry every inch of his perfect body, a body that is the essence of masculinity, with my tongue. I imagine my pointy pink tongue lingering in the crevice between his thigh and groin, slowly replacing crystal beads of moisture with thick swathes of saliva, before trailing up to his heavy balls, savoring the musky scent beneath the aroma of soap.

Despite the exhaust fan's best efforts, it never keeps pace with Dar's preferred scalding showers, and steam swirls around me when I enter. I close the door behind me and lean against it, watching Dar behind the wall of glass that separates the shower from the rest of the bathroom, being assaulted by the high pressure dual showerheads positioned at each end of the shower. He doesn't notice me, as he faces the back wall of the enclosure, allowing my gaze to fall to his muscular bottom. He scrubs himself as I silently watch. I'm filled with a mixture of admiration, thankfulness and lust as the muscles in his back ripple beneath his skin with each movement of his arms.

Despite my silence, something in the air must have changed, because he abruptly turns and sees me.

"Awake now, my lazy pet," he says.

"Dar, you didn't really want me to run with you. You know how frustrating it ends up for both of us."

"Wouldn't have asked you, Tess, if I didn't want your company," he replies, extending an arm from behind the wall of glass.

I walk toward him and he steps out of the water just far enough to grab me and pull me in.

"Dar, no, no, I'm in my robe," I say, realizing by now it's a moot point, it's soaked, I'm soaked and I don't care.

He lifts me and presses my back hard against the marble wall, still cool despite the heated water. My legs, crossed at the ankles, are tight around his waist. His hands are flat against the wall, my fingers interlaced together behind his neck. My chin falls into the hollow of his shoulder, my tongue trailing up to his ear, licking up the plump water droplets that define my path. I feel his cock stiffening against my pelvis and thoughts of him buried inside me make me nearly feral. I bite harder than I'd planned into his soft earlobe. He doesn't jerk away; he doesn't even move, but he whispers words that I barely have time to comprehend, "So you want to play rough, Tess?" before he's pushed me tighter against the wall with his hips. One of his large hands guides his cock into my ready cunt. A deep sigh, of relief, of satisfaction, is the last sound I make before both his hands are on my neck.

Fixing me in his dark gaze, his deep voice speaks softly, nearly drowned out between the dual cascades of water and the pulse beating a steady rhythm in my ears, "You should know by now, Tess, I repay pain with pain."

Even as his hands tighten on my throat, I can't take my eyes off his. I'm not sure what I hope to see in his stare. Sometimes he can go so cold that even while his eyes are fixed on mine, I know he's looking beyond me, looking somewhere into the darkness that resides so close to the edge of his surface civility. And sometimes, like now, I know he's watching me intently to gauge my reaction, and, as my breathing gets more and more impaired as he cuts off my respiration, to determine when to stop.

My fingers unlace, slide free of one another, desperately clutching at his neck. Somewhere in my oxygen-depleted brain, I know I'll have left deep crescent-shaped indentations and scratches where I claw at him. I'm terrified, and my mind won't stop shouting, *Not safe, this is not safe, you could die, he would never let you die, no, not safe, stop.* But I have no breath, I can't speak. My communication is limited to what he reads in my eyes and the pressure of my nails on his slick skin. When I have no air at all each thrust inside me feels even more intense. I know I could come; I feel the muscles in my cunt tightening around him, squeezing his erection as hard as my fingers dig into his neck. The lack of breath, the heat, his stare, the sensation of his cock hitting hard against my cervix, all these combined make me woozy, delirious. I can't breathe. *How long has it been? Not safe, not safe, not safe*, my brain shrieks.

Then, his eyes drift from mine for a moment and his words

enter my ear and echo in my head: "My breath will be the first air you taste, bitch. Come now; come when you feel my lips on yours. Come."

Dark brown eyes focus on mine again as his lips meet mine. My muscles pulsate wildly around his cock, squeezing him with a pressure that surpasses his on my throat. My eyelids flutter, my head falling back against the slick marble wall. The tight grip he has on my neck relents and as I gasp for air, his breath, seeming to have more substance than is possible, enters my mouth and fills my lungs. The return of my air feels like a gift he's bestowed upon me.

And with that returned air, my body goes limp, the combination of fear, stress and orgasm leaving me too spent to even cling to him any longer. He holds me up a few moments longer before allowing me to slide down the marble wall, making sure my legs will support me before releasing his hold. Against the wall, as I've been all along, I'm out of the direct spray from the showerhead, getting wet from the water that ricochets off Dar's body. With my robe open and slipping off my shoulders, I step into the stream, letting the water rain hard upon my upturned face. My thin sodden robe feels so weighty now that I slide it off my shoulders. Transfixed for a moment, I watch the water swirling rapidly down the drain.

Looking up, I see him watching me. "Oh, god, Dar," I whimper hoarsely, my throat still sore from the pressure.

"How appropriate that the first word you speak, spoken with my breath, should be god," he says. His face gives away nothing, impassive and utterly calm, as if he's entirely serious, but we both know that anytime he refers to himself as god, it will spur my irreverence.

"Yes, love, I exist solely because of you, for you," I reply with an eye roll any teenage girl would envy.

He pins me with a cool, dark glare, one that makes me think perhaps I've overstepped my bounds, before his large hands meet my shoulders and push me back against the wall once more.

"I don't think I can go through that again. Please, Dar, not right now," I say, in hopes of earning his compassion.

His face, so stern a moment ago, is now smiling, "Oh, yes, pet," he says, as he sinks to his knees, thick fingers opening my puffy folds, "I fully intend to take your breath away again."

LONG TIME GONE

Heidi Champa

The card had come in the mail weeks before, and I had ignored it. It had been ten years since graduation, and I had no desire to return and see what everyone was up to. The people I wanted to see, I saw. The rest, I avoided, like normal people do. But, despite my better judgment, I decided to attend anyway. Hell, it was free drinks and food. I would stay for a few hours and head home no worse for wear.

If I was honest, there was only one person I wanted to see there. One face, staring back at me from across the room. Even as I filled out the card to RSVP to the event, I knew there was little chance of that happening. Ethan was the last person I expected to see at a cheesy college reunion.

I had unofficially met Ethan soon after arriving at school, barely exchanging a few words. It was his touch that hooked me. From the outside, it looked incidental. As I stood on the outskirts of the group, I didn't notice a handcart full of books headed my way. I was too busy staring at him. Ethan pulled me out of the way, never missing a beat. His rough hands dug into my arms, and on one bicep, there was a thumb-shaped bruise the next day. I was fascinated. The tiny pinch of pain I felt every time I touched it caused my stomach to tighten and my heart to flutter. No kiss, no hand-holding had ever given me such a thrill. The bruise took over my mind. If a simple touch could leave me marked, what could he do if he really meant it?

We didn't speak until we wound up in the same Shakespeare class. He was older and cooler than all the boys I knew. I found myself staring at him all the time, willing him to turn and cast a glance my way. Finally, he did, out of the blue one day. No single glance had ever melted me more. I sat there, trying to maintain my composure. While I was listening to our professor lecture on the early pages of *Macbeth*, Ethan turned and glanced at me over his shoulder. His brown eyes bored into me, sending electricity all through my body. Several more times during the lecture, he stole looks. By the time I walked out, my panties were wet and I wanted to throw myself at him. Sense prevailed, at least for the time being. Soon enough, Ethan was talking to me. It couldn't be defined as meaningful conversation, but it served to stoke the desire I had for him. It wasn't until he touched me again that I truly understood what he did to me.

Our courtship was unconventional from the very start. There were no dates to speak of. The first time Ethan followed me to my room after class, there wasn't even a conversation. In mere seconds after his arrival, his hands were up my shirt, teasing my nipples. We made out on my bed for hours. He pinned my arms down as he sucked my neck, leaving my first hickey behind as evidence of his visit. More bruises followed from his strong and powerful hands, some on my legs, some on my arms, his fingers leaving evidence of his desire all over my body.

Things progressed quickly, at least the physical things. Our talks were short and perfunctory, just enough to keep things honest. But I couldn't recall one serious conversation that Ethan and I had shared. It was just part of a long list of things I couldn't recall. I did remember the first time I realized I would do anything he told me to do.

He had called to say he'd be coming to my room. He wanted me to be ready, but I got caught up studying, and I failed to be waiting on my bed when he arrived. My eyes widened behind my glasses when I saw his face. There was an intensity behind his eyes I had never experienced before. He walked toward me, grabbed the pen out of my hand and took the glasses from my face. Sliding my chair back hard, he pulled me up by my hand and led me toward the bed. Without a clue what would happen next, my heart was pounding as he pulled me hard across his lap. My pants and panties were down to the floor before a sound could come out of my mouth in protest.

"I told you to be ready when I got here. What were you doing?"

I swallowed hard as I hesitated to answer his question. Before I had formed the words in my throat, I felt it—the rush of air heading toward my exposed ass, the surge of heat and pain that jolted through me as his hand hit my skin with more force than I had ever experienced. The sound echoed off the walls, the crack slowly dissipating into the cement block that surrounded us.

"What were you doing?" His voice was deeper this time, making me shake, not with fear but with anticipation of what was to come.

"Studying. I was studying." The words tumbled out of my mouth, my breath ragged and fast. His hand rubbed lightly over my flesh. It felt so hot, alive. I was aware, for the first time, of how wet my cunt was. The lips were rubbing together, slick with the moisture a single strike of his hand had caused. His fingers teased me, but I needed more. I was waiting for more.

"Being ready for me doesn't mean studying. It means being in this bed and being wet. I specifically asked you to be naked. Didn't I?"

Again I hesitated. Part of me did it on purpose, to see if I could elicit the same response. I did. The second spank was as hard as the first, sending my moans ringing through the room. He followed it quickly with two more slaps on my now-burning flesh. The pain mixed with the swirling pleasure in my mind, and I knew in that moment I wanted more. I wanted him to spank me again and again. I felt another rush of air, and I closed my eyes, waiting for the next hit. But instead, he stopped before he hit me, choosing instead to run a finger down the crack of my ass. My skin felt bright red, the blood close to the surface trying to escape.

The gentle stroke of his finger lulled me until I relaxed. Just as I did, he grabbed a handful of my hair and pulled my head back hard. His face was next to mine, his breath sweet and moist on my face.

"You like that, don't you? You like it when I spank you."

"Yes. I like it." I couldn't lie. There was no way I could tell him I didn't love it. But he already knew; he just wanted to make me say it out loud. To me, my words rang just as loudly against the walls as the spanks had. Never in my life did I imagine I would admit to something like that.

"I could tell from the moment I saw you that you needed it. You walk around just begging for it. The first time I looked at that ass, I knew I needed to spank it." His fingers found their way to my dripping cunt, sliding inside without a moment of resistance. As he fingered me, he went back to work, spanking my ass in a syncopated rhythm while his fingers stayed steady and slow. The pain blurred so perfectly with the pleasure, mixing into such a heady cocktail of need inside me. Just when I thought I couldn't take one more hit, he stopped, his hand still in midair.

"Get up and take off your shirt." I stood, shaky on my feet, and removed my shirt. He stood in front of me, his hands sliding over my skin, missing my nipples completely. His hands pushed down on my shoulders until I was kneeling in front of him. I waited for him to give me his cock, but instead his fingers, wet from my pussy, slid into my mouth. Ethan made me suck each of his three fingers clean, smirking as I licked myself off his thick digits. His hands once again grabbed my hair, tugging until I had to cry out with the pain of it.

"From now on, you'll do what I say, won't you?"

"Yes."

"Say it again."

"Yes. I'll do what you say."

He pulled on my hair harder. In that moment, with my mouth agape, his cock slid inside my mouth, silencing me.

Ethan fucked me so hard that day, I could barely stand after he left. My ass went black and blue for three days. My wrists bore the red marks of the scarves he'd used to tie me to the bed. I walked around all over campus with the badge of Ethan on me. No one ever knew what went on in that room. Or that it went on for years after that. I dated other guys, fooled around. But Ethan was the only one who really knew what I wanted.

The night of the reunion was exactly as I expected. A random banquet room, filled with mostly strange faces. The few people I recognized made quick work of finding me, despite my hiding near a corner. After twenty minutes of useless mingling, I saw him across the room, looking just as good as he ever had. Ethan. He wasn't an old boyfriend. He wasn't even a friend. He was the best fuck I had ever had, the only guy who ever gave me what I truly wanted and needed. He was right across the room, sipping beer and talking to some nameless stranger. His eyes scanned the room, moving right over me and not even stopping. Just like before, just like the old days, he was going to ignore me until he was good and ready to see me.

In that ballroom, Ethan was a mythical figure surrounded by mere mortals. I still couldn't believe my eyes. I willed him to look at me, just like I had in that class. I knew he had seen me, but his eyes never locked on mine. I clutched my wineglass and followed him all over the room with my gaze. Finally, after more schmoozing and laughter, Ethan turned and faced me. His eyes burned into mine, and the rest of the room seemed to drift away. He didn't smile, didn't even register my face. But, I knew. I knew he remembered me.

My heart nearly stopped as he strode toward me, and I tried my best to act casual. Sipping my drink and looking away, I felt Ethan brush against me. I expected him to keep going, but he stopped, pretending to look at an old yearbook next to me on the table. I felt him press something into my hand, and I flooded with heat as he walked away, leaving the scent of his cologne behind. I couldn't breathe. Finding the bathroom, I went into and locked the stall, finally feeling safe enough to open my hand and see what Ethan had given me. It was a plastic room key and a tiny piece of paper. I unfolded it, and read: *Room 1534, 15 minutes*. My body shuddered. Ethan wanted me in his room in fifteen minutes. Detouring back to the reunion, I quickly downed two shots of vodka. I needed a little courage, even though I was desperate for this moment. It had been so long since I had felt Ethan's touch, so long since I had found anyone who was willing to give me exactly what I needed. With Ethan, I didn't need to tell him. I strode to the elevator, trembling and quaking inside, my face already flushed with excitement.

I slid the card key into the lock, waiting for the green flash to appear and signal me into the room. The cool air hit me as the door swung open, and I saw the room, dark and untouched. The only sign of Ethan was a suitcase on a chair across the room. If I closed my eyes, I could smell him. My mind was on overload, waiting for Ethan to come. The hands of my watch moved so slowly, I couldn't take it. I sat on the edge of the bed, tapping my foot quickly to try and get the nervousness out of me, but there was no way to shake the feeling I had. Ethan had left me changed all those years ago. There was no way to stop the intense mix of fear, anticipation, lust and excitement coursing through my body at that moment.

Finally, I heard steps in the hallway, the click of plastic in the door lock. I held my breath as Ethan emerged through the doorjamb, his stride confident. The room remained dark and the shadows that fell across his face made him look rough and dangerous. His hand reached out and stroked down the side of my face. I closed my eyes at the feeling of his touch, so gentle and sure. I was hot under my clothes, and I squirmed against the hard mattress.

"I was surprised to see you here." His voice was just as low and hard as I remembered. His finger ran over my lips and down to my chin as I looked up at him. He cut such an imposing figure, just looking at him was flooding me with wetness.

"I wasn't going to come, Ethan, but I figured what the hell."

His hand lowered back to his side, the familiar smirk played across his lips.

"Don't lie. You came here hoping to see me, didn't you? Tell me."

Unable to manage actual words, I just nodded. I couldn't lie to him. In my secret thoughts, I had hoped and prayed for this very moment, for Ethan to take me to his room and bend me over his knee. But in reality, I never thought I'd be sitting here, waiting for him to make his move.

"Get up. Let me look at you."

I did as I was told, rising to my feet slowly. He scanned me up and down, stopping to stare at my barest hint of cleavage. Never having had large breasts, I had managed to rustle them together for the evening. My skirt was short, but not too short. Finally, his eyes rested on my high heels, black and strappy. He stepped toward me, pushing my hair back from my eyes. Just as I relaxed into his touch, his hand tightened in my hair, pulling my head back harshly. Crying out into the dark room, I relished the pain, feeling the familiar surge of heat between my legs in response.

"After all these years, still such a bad girl. God, I can't wait to turn that ass black and blue."

I gasped again as his hand tightened a bit more. His eyes were bright, even in the dim light. He grinned, releasing my hair. He turned me roughly so that my hands landed on the bed to steady myself. Ethan kicked my feet apart, pushing my skirt up my thighs. His hands ran up from my knees, moving my skirt up to my waist. The only things between us now were my panty hose and thong, both wet from my pussy. I could feel him behind me, and I waited, waited for anything to happen. His hands ran over my ass, smoothing over the nylon that covered my trembling flesh. Suddenly, I felt the material ripping and tearing away from my skin. The sound rang violently off the walls, filling the silence that had set in between us. I could feel my panty hose in tatters at my ankles; the only pieces not in shreds were inside my shoes. Lord knows what became of my thong, as it too was long gone. My ass was now exposed, the cool air of the room raising goose bumps on my skin. I knew his eyes were on me, devouring me. But I needed to feel his hands; I needed him to touch me.

My hands dug into the bed, and I nearly jumped when I felt his hand come to rest on the small of my back. The other traced lazy circles across my skin, teasing me just like he used to. I held my breath and closed my eyes. Time stood still for the next few seconds. And then the familiar rush of air preceded the exquisite burst of pain. It took all I had not to scream out, to fall forward on the bed from the force. It was as if ten years of pent-up energy landed on my ass in that spank.

Before I could get my composure back, two more spanks followed and this time the scream did come. I didn't care who else in the hotel could hear me, I couldn't contain the feelings anymore. I could feel my wetness on my thighs and a slight sweat breaking out on my forehead. The spanks kept coming, in his unusual rhythm. By this time, I had lost count of how many times his hand lit up my flesh, burning my ass with each powerful hit. My heart was pounding and I could feel the sting of tears in the corners of my eyes. Suddenly, he stopped. I felt, for the first time, how my flesh tingled and radiated heat.

"Stand up." I moved away from the bed. I turned and saw him setting his tie aside, his jacket already off. His fingers then moved to my blouse, making quick work of the buttons. He stripped me naked, replacing my shoes after the panty hose were gone. He walked toward his suitcase, leaving me standing naked by the bed. He turned, and a pair of silver handcuffs glittered in the dark.

"You don't mind if we don't go back to the reunion, do you? We have a lot of catching up to do."

I didn't answer; I knew I didn't need to. He came to me, grabbing the scorched flesh of my ass roughly. He shoved me down on the bed, face-first. I listened as the soft click of the cuffs closed around my wrists. Ten years and nothing had changed. He still knew exactly what I needed.

POWER
OVER POWER

Emerald

I pulled open the glass door against the glaring Saturday morning sun. The heavily windowed walls offered little relief from its brightness as I blinked and looked around the lobby.

Dominic sat at his desk across from the front counter. One month before, I had watched Dominic on the first night of class as he stood at the front of the studio and introduced the defense system in which he would be training us. The students stood in a row in front of him, dressed the same way he was in sneakers, black T-shirts with the royal blue KRAV MAGA logo on the chest, and loose, lightweight black pants with matching royal blue stripes down the sides.

"Krav Maga is not like traditional martial arts," he had explained. "Traditional martial arts involve sparring, a back-and-forth, a focus on skill. Krav Maga is about dropping somebody—knocking someone out within ten seconds so you can get away." He met the eyes of each student in the line in front of him. "It's also not about size. The point of Krav is that it puts everyone on an equal playing field, focusing on universal vulnerabilities that anyone can exploit, regardless of size."

His voice was calm, assured, serious. I had watched him, captivated. Dominic didn't necessarily look like a self-defense expert. He was only slightly taller than I was, probably five foot ten. His build was slim and athletic. The denseness of his muscles, however, was evident not only under the short sleeves of his T-shirt but also in the resounding thuds that reverberated off the studio walls as he demonstrated kicks and punches, and used knees and elbows on the punching bag at the front of the room as the students watched in silence.

Despite the subject matter, there was no bravado or machismo in his countenance. I had seen from the pictures and accompanying labels hanging in the lobby that Dominic instructed in traditional martial arts as well as Krav Maga. While I had never taken any myself, I sensed in him the understated confidence I had observed before in martial artists—an exquisite self-possession and understanding of their capabilities, the assurance that there was no need to prove anything to anyone. It was like they had power over their own power. It served them rather than the other way around. There was no compulsion to use it, to put it on display; it was just there, second nature, if it was ever needed.

Dominic looked up at my entrance.

"Hi, Jackie."

I smiled at him and glanced at the clock. Saturday morning class was optional, a makeup class for those who missed any of the three sessions held during the week or who just wanted an extra review. I was only about five minutes early, but there didn't seem to be anyone else around.

He followed my gaze. "You're the only one here so far. People often trickle in around starting time on Saturdays. You can have a seat if you want, or go on in and start warming up."

I sat on the bench perpendicular to his desk, and he smiled and turned back to his computer. I didn't need to look at Dominic to feel the way he was affecting me. It happened just from being in the same room with him. It was something that went beyond looks, beyond personality, beyond simple attraction. It was pure heat, like a raw power of undiluted wanting, craving, hunger. I felt it when I watched the nonchalance with which he taught the methodology used by the Israeli army for hand-to-hand combat, a methodology designed, ultimately, to kill people. I watched the skill, control, and focus of the lightning flashes of movement, the cracking thuds that seemed effortless to him, and felt the raw heat in my core. Every movement he executed was exactly what was called for, nothing more, nothing less. He didn't execute power just for the sake of executing power. Power was cultivated in him so deeply that it simply came out when needed.

I wanted to fuck him so badly I could hardly stand still.

Five minutes later he glanced at the clock again. "Hmm. Maybe people had a little too much partying on a Friday night," he chuckled as he stood up. "I've never had attendance this low on a Saturday."

"Yeah, I imagine you want to cancel," I babbled, standing nervously.

Dominic shrugged. "It's up to you. You can certainly take off if you'd like. If you want to stay, I'll work you."

A shiver went through me, and I tried not to shudder visibly. I glanced around, not sure if I *did* want to take the class with Dominic all by myself. I knew his focus was strictly professional, and I might end up making a fool of myself as I practically drooled over him.

"Uh, okay. If you don't mind," I responded, my mouth appearing to ignore all the considerations that had just run through my mind.

"No, come on in," he said, indicating the studio with a jerk of his head and leading me into it. I moved to the far end toward the supply room and set my bag and purse down on the bench.

As we began stretching, my breath quickened. The training hadn't even begun, and already I knew this was a mistake. I wasn't going to be able to handle this kind of undivided attention from Dominic. Even if he were interested in what I was, which I had no reason to believe he was, the studio's walls were made of glass, making the view from the street wide open. He wasn't about to fuck me with that kind of visibility.

I had to get out of there.

"Okay, you remember the way we learned early in the week to defend against a choke hold?" Dominic asked.

"Yeah," I answered, clearing my throat. Dominic approached me, and I almost backed up, not trusting myself if he touched me.

"Show me what you remember." He reached forward and placed both hands around my neck, facing me. My breath caught, and I snapped my hands up and slammed my forearms into his, breaking the grip.

"Good," he said, stepping back. "Let's try it up against the wall."

I was painfully aware of my ragged breathing and the wetness between my legs as Dominic leaned into me, wrapping his hands around my neck and pushing me back against the wall. I defended again and had to consciously resist pressing my hand between my legs.

"Okay, grab a kick shield," Dominic said, nodding at a stack in the corner of the room. "I'm going to demonstrate the kick we learned on Wednesday. Remember, start with your weight on the kicking foot—hop quickly to the other foot and kick while you're in the air. The momentum increases your power. Then recoil immediately. Always recoil right away. Limbs not up against you are vulnerable to being grabbed."

I nodded, trying to focus. Dominic backed up, and I crouched in position with the kick pad in front of me. Dominic's foot snapped forward, and I was almost knocked backward by the force of the impact even as the padding absorbed most of it. I shuddered as I imagined what such a blow would be like without the shield.

"Your turn," Dominic took the pad from me.

I did my best to kick the sexual frustration out of me as I slammed first my right then my left foot into the kick pad with a grunt. I alternated back and forth until Dominic told me to stop.

The elevated heart rate and adrenaline pumping through me had not served the desired purpose at all.

"Do you remember the series we learned earlier in the week?" Dominic demonstrated in the air the series of punches, kicks, and elbow slams to get out of a headlock and render the assailant to the ground. I nodded.

"Okay, let's try it." Dominic fitted his arm around my neck from behind and held firmly. My breath caught, and I almost pressed back against him. I caught myself and mimed the series, stopping each move just short of actual impact with him. My breath was ragged when I finished. The tingling in my pussy had reached the point of distraction.

"Are you okay?" Dominic asked.

"Yeah," I squeaked out, almost wincing at the hoarseness of my voice. I cleared my throat. "Fine. Go right ahead," I said, managing to make my voice sound almost normal.

He turned me around and grabbed me around the neck again, and immediately I couldn't breathe—and it wasn't because his hold was too strong. I started the series, slamming my elbow back toward his chest, halting right before it made contact with him. Suddenly I forgot the next move and stopped.

"Don't stop," Dominic said. "Don't ever stop, Jackie."

"I forgot the next move," I stared to explain as Dominic turned me around.

"I know you did. But you're training yourself all the time here, and you don't ever want to train yourself to pause or freeze. If you forget what you're doing"—his eyes were serious as they penetrated mine—"just start throwing punches."

I held his gaze and managed to nod.

He backed up. "You want to grab some water?"

I nodded again and walked over to my bag as he moved to the side of the room to put the kick shield back. I took a drink, facing the bench, and set my water bottle down.

Suddenly a body was up against me from behind, arm rough around my neck. I was in a headlock. It took me just a second to realize I needed to defend myself, and I snapped an elbow back and tried to whirl, realizing it was too late.

Dominic whipped me around and pressed me against the wall. "Okay, you weren't expecting me there. You weren't ready, and you paused. *Assailants don't wait until you're ready.* You have to be prepared all the time." He eased his hold on me and backed up. I was breathless, staring in his eyes as my pussy tingled insistently.

"I'm going to grab some gloves," he said, moving to the supply room a few feet away.

He opened the door and disappeared through it as I stared at it. I swallowed. As if drawn by a magnet, my feet began to step toward the supply room. The door was open, and I could hear Dominic rummaging around inside as I approached. I reached the door and silently stepped through it.

Dominic had his back to me. He pulled a pair of gloves from the top of a pile and turned, stopping when he saw me.

I was already in the room, where I wasn't supposed to be. There was no way to back out gracefully now. For a few seconds there was silence.

"I want you to—" my voice, already tiny and faltering, failed me after those four words.

Dominic took a step forward, his expression questioning. He raised his eyebrows and cocked an ear toward me. "You want what?"

My breathing was uneven; I felt like I did when I was already close to orgasm. The intensity wasn't lending itself to articulation. I moved forward as well.

"I want," my voice halted again, but this time only for a split second. "I want you to fuck me."

I whispered it, knowing I was barely audible, and looked down at the ground, my cheeks flaming. I felt Dominic's eyes on me and told myself the worst he could do was say no, and I could turn around and leave and never come back. The all-encompassing fixation of wanting him overruled humiliation in me as the room stayed silent for a few seconds.

Dominic's motions were deliberate as he moved toward and then past me. My eyes widened. I didn't move.

The door closed. The quiet, solid thud as I sensed that he was still in the room with me sent a jolt of heat through me that almost made me dizzy. I barely breathed as I started to turn around.

But he was already back in front of me. He moved in so that he was almost touching me, close enough that I felt weak, but not actually making contact. He looked down at me.

"You want me to fuck you," he repeated. His tone was neutral.

I trembled, wanting to touch him but feeling frozen. Still

looking at the ground, I nodded.

With characteristic efficiency of motion, he reached with one finger and pulled my chin up. A shudder ran through me as I felt his power—the power I saw in every move he made, that he exuded at the front of the class, that he spoke when he told us what we were capable of, that coiled and expelled from him whenever he slammed any part of his body into the punching bag. This was the power that lived unquestioned within him, so seamlessly that it was as though it wouldn't exist without him.

I moved my eyes to his. Dominic pushed forward and kissed me, hard, his body pressing against mine as I hit the wall behind me. I thrashed against him, my hands ripping at his T-shirt as I fought to breathe. I felt like I could already come.

Dominic placed a hand behind my neck and gripped my waist, pulling my body even closer to his. I pulled at his shirt again and he let go of me and stripped it off, reaching to pull mine off as well before returning his hands to the solid grip of my body and my mouth to his unrelenting kiss. I could feel his erection against me as he slowed down and eased back.

"We'd need a condom," he whispered, looking down at me.

My eyes felt out of focus as I looked back at him. "I have some in my purse," I whispered back, barely recognizing my own voice.

Dominic stepped back, and I walked shakily to the door in my pants, sneakers, and sports bra. I opened it and stepped through, blinking at the sunlight streaming in through the glass walls. It felt like a different world.

I retrieved my purse and reentered the supply room unsteadily. As I stepped through the door, Dominic's hard chest hit me from behind, his arm instantaneously around my neck. I drew a quick breath and rammed my elbow to within an inch of his chest, my own chest heaving.

He whirled me around and pushed me back up against the wall.

"Good reaction time that time," he said, his voice low. "Particularly under the circumstances." I felt the hardness of his cock pressing against my hip. Slowly, he brought one hand up to grip my throat, then the other to join it.

"You know what to do now?" His voice was a whisper. The question wasn't really a question. We had just practiced it in the studio.

I nodded. He looked at me, not moving.

"I don't want to," I whispered. I heard the tremble in my voice.

Dominic nodded slowly, eyes still on mine. He could have held me in place with them alone. He moved one hand to stroke a finger along my jawline, his eyes following it. His other hand stayed in place at my throat. He licked his lips and looked back at me.

Suddenly his grip tightened as he lifted me up against the wall by my neck. My jaw dropped, feet hanging loosely without the ground beneath them. I was exactly at eye level with Dominic now, his hand against the sides of my neck in a way that somehow barely hurt.

My pussy started to drip.

Dominic's eyes blazed into mine as he reached and ran a finger from my collarbone down to the top of my sports bra. Slowly he lowered me back to the ground and pushed my sports bra up, grabbing my breasts with a firmness just short of painful. My breath came to a fiery halt in my throat.

"Breathe," he whispered, looking into my eyes. It was an order he often gave during class. I obeyed, expelling the breath caught in my throat and deliberately guiding in another one.

Dominic reached up and removed my ponytail holder, then

yanked my bra over my head and pulled me forward. He guided me across the room to a stack of floor mats about waist high. Pressing me up against them, he ran his hand up the back of my neck and grabbed my hair near my scalp. I whimpered as he kissed me, involuntarily gyrating against him. He lowered his hands and yanked my pants and panties down to my knees, lifting me to the stack of mats and pulling them the rest of the way off almost before I realized what was happening. I kicked my sneakers off and looked at him, breathing heavily.

Dominic lifted me back to the ground and turned me around, one hand holding my hip, the other tracing lightly over the front of my body. His fingers strayed casually, rising over the swell of my breast, dragging lightly across the nipple, then down the other side and on to the next one. The reminder to breathe was gone. I felt like I had forgotten how.

I wanted him to throw me down, ram his cock into me and fuck me hard, take full control of me, of him, of—everything. I tried to wiggle impatiently and realized that despite the calmness of his movements, the grip he had on me was like a clothespin on tissue paper. I felt his breath on my ear, steady in comparison to my almost frantic panting. Slowly he moved his hand from my breasts to the back of my neck again, sliding up through my hair and gripping into a fist. I caught my breath.

"Well, conveniently enough, I want to fuck you, too, Jackie," he whispered smoothly, and my legs trembled. "And I think I know what you want me to do. You want me to hold you down, fuck you hard, get pretty rough with you." I wondered if, for the first time, I would come without actually being touched. "You're looking for power. In your own way, getting fucked rough like that will make you feel powerful. Is that right?" My vision was becoming fuzzy, and I could hardly make sense of the words he was saying.

Dominic let go of my hip and slid his hand across my stomach, up over my breasts and finally to my throat.

"Everything you're looking for, Jackie, you already have inside you." The tone of his whisper had changed, and I barely had time to process the words before he whipped me around, forcing my mouth open with his as he kissed me again. He held my hair in a fist of steel and moved his other hand back to my body, lightly brushing my rib cage. He pulled away and I watched the slow movement of his fingers, gliding like honey running over my skin.

I whimpered desperately. He hadn't even touched my pussy, and I felt close to a kind of climax of which I didn't know the meaning. It felt like a near euphoria combined with a vague but deep fear that together seemed to be pushing tears seriously toward the surface.

"Dominic," I pleaded. My voice trembled like a blade of grass in the breeze. He looked up at me.

I realized then what he was doing. He was making me wait, making me feel, making me experience every single nuance, every detail, everything that was in me, in my body, rather than slamming it all away.

And suddenly I wondered if that was what having power over power meant.

The tears flowed out of me like an orgasm, fully beyond my control, my breath turning to a silent sob that felt somehow calm, even peaceful, as I felt a space open up in me I wasn't sure I had ever felt before. Dominic's eyes stayed on mine.

The wave moved through me, and Dominic dropped his finger to my clit. I gasped and climaxed as soon as he moved it, orgasm bursting forth in a rush so overpowering I almost felt I would lose consciousness. Steady, unabated screams pulsed through me as Dominic held my gaze as well as my balance with his unyielding grip at my neck. When it was done I fell limp, my entire body slick with sweat, legs shaking and hanging like string over the stack of mats.

Dominic lowered me onto my back and let go of my hair, then backed up and retrieved my purse. Hands shaking, I reached and fumbled through it in my horizontal position until I found the little zippered pouch. Extracting a condom from it, I pushed it into his hand.

I heard the package rip open and my purse drop to the floor as Dominic backed up. He slid me up farther on the stack of mats and leapt lightly onto them, pushing between my legs. My eyes were closed, and I opened them as he hovered above me. I was far beyond words, knowing only what was in my body.

"Breathe," Dominic whispered again as he dropped his body onto mine, plunging into me and grasping my shoulders as his breath rushed against my ear. He thrust into me with rhythmic strength as I lay like a doll, sprawled powerlessly across the hard foam beneath me. Dominic pumped hard, holding my hips solidly. His breathing changed as he thrust just a bit harder and came inside me, my body like a deflated balloon, a beautiful, motionless receptacle for his come.

I closed my eyes again as he finished, feeling a sorrow at the impending loss of contact with his body. When he pulled out, I opened my eyes and turned to him. He leapt off the stack of mats and reached to help me down. I stopped at the edge, not ready to stand up yet.

In a daze, I looked at the floor, my body shaking. Dominic's low voice broke the silence.

"Whatever is in you, whatever you're feeling—feel it. Don't hide from it. Don't try to 'beat' it. Be with it until you understand it, until you know where it comes from." I frowned at the floor. "Then it won't rule you anymore."

I raised my eyes to his as he finished the sentence. Sweat dripped from my forehead onto my neck as my quick breaths punctuated the silence in the room.

"That's what power is," Dominic said. "It doesn't have anything to do with force or subjugation."

I looked down at his hand as he held it out to me again and allowed my body to slide off the mats. My feet on the floor felt foreign.

I gathered my clothes and dressed slowly. Dominic handed me my purse as I straightened, and we walked to the door together. I turned to him; without a word, he grabbed the back of my neck and kissed me, rendering me immediately breathless as I braced myself against the door with one hand.

He let go of me slowly. My hand slipped from the door as he took a step back.

"See you Monday." Dominic's hand brushed the small of my back once before he stepped forward and turned the knob.

KNOT HERE!

Yolanda West

H ere?" I try to keep my voice low, but I'm caught by surprise.

John's answer is nonverbal. The corners of his eyes crinkle, he nods slightly, the ends of his handlebar mustache edge upward with his grin.

We're at a diner off Highway 42, halfway to his mom's house to celebrate her birthday. He'd said he had something special planned for the trip, but I thought it was the beads.

Oh, yes. The beads. There are four of them strung together, made of hollow plastic, a bit smaller than ben wa balls, with heavy steel marbles inside them. The whole lot is inside me, held in place by my panties, shifting and quaking with every movement.

It's funny. When we first met, John was so shy about his sexuality that he was nervous about doing the things he wanted to do to me even in his own place. He'd been brought up in a very conservative household and had never expressed his urges until he met me.

I'd been with several doms and had come away disillusioned. I wasn't even looking for anyone when I met John through a friend of a friend, but the chemistry was immediate. I dated him in "vanilla mode" for a while, but I was afraid to fall for him if I was going to have to suppress my own submissiveness.

So one day, I just blurted it out. "Tie me up," I said. I'll never forget the look on his face. He stuttered and stammered and said he didn't think he could. But I'd seen the look. I knew it all too well. A man who has bondage in his blood gets a certain look when he imagines binding a girl, and John definitely had that look.

And he wasn't bad at it, for a guy who had no actual "hands-on" experience. It was obvious he'd studied plenty of pictures and was also handy with a rope from being a Boy Scout.

The result was electric. That first time may have been tame on the surface, but as soon as he had me tied to his bed, he transformed into the most masterful lover I'd ever had. Reading my body, my reactions, was second nature to him. It was heaven.

Still, he remained shy about it for a long time. He needed encouragement to come out of his shell. I suppose some of what I did then could be considered topping from the bottom, but sometimes, a girl's gotta do what a girl's gotta do.

That phase didn't last long, though. He lost his shyness quickly and even went to some workshops with me. But whenever I suggested we try some public kinkiness, he had steadfastly refused—until today.

So it was only natural for me to assume that the beads were the extent of our "public" adventure. Except that now, as we're sitting here in the diner, he brings out the rope.

It's just one short length of nylon cord. He lays it on the table and then reaches across and takes my wrists. I'm already wet from the beads, and the way he grips me almost sends me over the edge right then and there. In fact, he has to tighten his hold to keep me from sliding under the table.

A shadow falls across the table. Our waitress has arrived. She's fortyish, plump, looks bored with everything, has seen it all. "Hi, my name's Justine, I'll be your server," she chants, monotone, then stops short, noticing the way John is holding on to me. "Are you all right, deary?"

I don't trust myself to open my mouth, so I nod and attempt a smile. She glances at John and then back to me. She shrugs, skeptical, but not alarmed.

John perks up. "'Justine,' huh? DeSade wrote a book called *Justine*. Did you know that?"

She looks puzzled, then annoyed at the pop quiz. "Look," she says with a heavy sigh, "do you need more time to decide?"

"No, we're very ready," John says, winking at me.

"Wait!" says Justine with a sudden sign of life. "Didn't he make cars or something, like, way back?"

Now John is puzzled. "Who?"

"DeSoto."

John and I both stifle a laugh. "Yes," he says, "I think that's right."

"So, what'll it be then?" she asks, addressing me first.

My attention is on John's hands holding on to me. Carefully forming my words, I ask for a salad only. Justine scribbles and recites the choice of dressings. I nod when she comes to ranch.

She turns expectantly to John, but he's looking straight at me. "Switch," he says to me.

Shit. I'm sitting with my legs crossed, right over left. Switching to left over right forces the beads to shift around within their steamy alcove. "Oh!" I gasp. "Mm," I sigh.

Justine looks back at me. "You sure you're okay?"

John speaks up. "Justine, we're on our way to my mother's house, so what I want is a nice grilled cheese sandwich, just like Mom used to make when I was a boy. Good ol' American cheese between two slices of white bread, buttered and toasted on a hot griddle till the cheese oozes from the sides. And be sure the cook smashes it down real good with a greasy spatula, too."

Justine rolls her eyes. "A number three," she mutters, jotting it down on her pad.

As she saunters away, John loops the rope around my wrists. I can't believe he's actually doing it. I sit mesmerized as he forms the square knot and pulls it tight.

Under the table, his foot pushes against my crossed leg. Obeying his silent command, I put both feet on the floor and spread them apart for him. Soon his foot is up my skirt, between my thighs, nudging against my...my...

"John!" The word erupts louder than expected.

"Yes, Annie?" he says, ever so smoothly. He smiles as he tightens his grip on my bound wrists.

I try to sit still, but can't help squirming. I keep my mouth closed, but can't help moaning. I'm panting and sweating, as if I'd just sprinted a few blocks. I hang my head and close my eyes, and pray no one notices us.

It's happening and there's nothing I can do about it. The first shudder starts deep within me and quickly spreads throughout. Another follows immediately.

"Oh! God! Shit!" And to think I'm the one who wanted this.

I can see how much John is loving it now. The teasing and tormenting is so much more intense in public. And then I realize why he chose today. It's precisely because we're on the way to his mom's house, where his conservative family will be, especially his starched-shirt brother and prissy sister-in-law. I think he's enjoying the contrast between them and his own wanton slut.

Justine returns with our orders. I try to tuck my hands under the table, but she sees the rope around my wrists and glares at John.

He shrugs. "She has a condition," he says. "Seizures. Convulsions. It's necessary to control her sometimes."

"Uh-huh," says Justine.

She glances in my direction, but I'm occupied with trying to guide a forkful of lettuce to my mouth. It's no easy task with my hands tied and John's foot still in my crotch. She clears her throat to speak. "Something to drink?"

John picks that exact instant to give my pussy an extra little push.

"No!" I snap, way too loudly.

"Fine. Suit yourself." She walks away and begins whispering to some of the patrons at the counter.

We finish as much of our food as we can. I know John is excited, too. I can almost see his hard-on through the look in his eyes. Leaving my hands tied, he gets up to pay the bill. I follow along, walking gingerly. The beads are doing such a number on me, I'm sucking air with each step to keep from crying out.

Once outside, John puts his arm around me and guides me to the back of the diner. The small building is on a lonely stretch of road, with only a patch of woods behind it.

He brightens as we round the corner of the building and I immediately see why. He takes my hands and pulls them high over my head. There's a convenient hook on the back of the building, which he puts to good use. It's a bit of a stretch, but my toes stay in contact with the ground. I wonder when he noticed that?

He kisses me furiously as I half dangle there. His hands rove possessively up and down my body. I can finally feel his cock straining for release. I can't believe we're actually going to do it right here. But I want it. I want it!

"Oh, god, John, hurry!" I gasp.

He tears himself away just long enough to raise my skirt, rip my panties off and yank the beads from their warm niche. He shoves my things in his pocket, then unzips. His beautiful cock springs out, eager for action.

He grabs my ass to support me as I lift my legs and wrap them around his waist. And then he's in me, ramming and slamming me against the wall.

It's over so fast I hardly notice the strain on my arms. He lingers for a moment, then withdraws. He substitutes fingers for cock and does a thorough job of probing my depths and stimulating my clit. I can hardly keep from screaming, but his other hand, quickly clamped over my mouth, helps.

I forget where we are and just let go, coming for him, my body doing his bidding: so delicious.

At last, he pulls the beads from his pocket and eases them back inside me. Then he slips my hands from the hook and unties the rope. He hands me my panties and I pull them back on.

As I follow him on wobbly legs back to the car, we find Justine at the side of the building. She's smoothing out her skirt. Her face is flushed. It's obvious she's been watching us. She's been watching and masturbating.

There's an awkward silence, then she smiles and shrugs. "Next time," she says, "just leave a bigger tip."

VERONICA'S BODY

Isabelle Gray

Veronica has a past. She refuses to talk about it. Veronica is married to Vince. Vince is a particular man. He likes what he likes, wants what he wants. When he's unhappy Veronica is unhappy. He doesn't ask about her past. She does whatever it takes to make him happy. It is a mutually beneficial arrangement.

At night, Veronica sleeps chained to the bed she shares with her husband. Her slender wrists are cuffed together and then locked to the canopy above with a long length of chain, the better for her to sleep. Just before midnight, Veronica washes her face, brushes her teeth, performs her other evening ablutions. She dabs a bit of perfume on the points of her collarbone. As she goes through her routine, her stomach flutters and a flush of heat starts crawling across her skin. When she's ready, she takes a deep breath, slips out of her silk robe and lies on the bed where Vince is waiting. He stretches himself along her body, covering her thighs with his, the hair on his legs tickling her. Slowly, he drags his fingers between her thighs, traces her pussy lips, presses his hand against her mound, then up her torso, flat and firm. As he lowers his lips to her breasts, she gasps, every time. He sinks his teeth into each nipple, rolls the soft flesh between hard enamel. He kisses the hollow at the base of her throat, the tip of her chin, her armpits. He licks lazy circles along the undersides of her arms. Finally, he places a moist kiss on each inner wrist before fastening the cuffs around them and chaining his wife to the bed. He tells her to sleep well. He turns off the light and settles in next to his wife, a possessive arm draped across her stomach. He falls asleep smiling.

It doesn't matter if she's tired or not. Come midnight, Veronica knows that her place is in bed, by her husband's side. When they travel, the cuffs come with them. On the nights she can't sleep, Veronica lies in the dark, staring at the ceiling or out at the night sky, enjoying the mild ache in her arms, eyes wide open. She has lived a lot of her life with her eyes wide open.

Sometimes, a few hours after she has fallen asleep, Veronica feels her husband climb atop her, his cock hard and insistently throbbing against her thighs. She knows what to do. She spreads her legs, wide. As Vince buries his cock inside his wife, stretching her open, she moans drowsily. She doesn't have to move or groan or call out his name. She only has to allow herself to be used. It turns her on that in the dark of their bedroom, their bodies heavy with sleep, she is just a tight warm space from which her husband will extract his satisfaction. She is always wet and ready for him. Vince fucks her hard at night, moaning with each thrust of his hips, squeezing his fingers roughly into her thighs, leaving coin-sized bruises for her to admire in the morning.

Veronica has a life of her own, a successful career. She works long hours, keeps her own money. But she is always available to her husband. When he comes to her workplace with that look in his eye, his chin set to the right, she knows to close her office

door behind him. She knows to speak only when spoken to, to
fall to her knees, cross her ankles, bow her head. She stares at the
shine of his shoes, the fine cut of his slacks. She bows her head
lower, until she is prostrate. She lovingly kisses each of his shoes.
She stays like that until she hears the zipper of his slacks slowly
being lowered. He wraps his fingers in her long red hair, curling them into a tight fist. He pulls her head up, drags his thumb
across her lower lip, then slides his thumb into her mouth. She
sucks on it, loudly, sloppily. He opens her mouth wider and says,
"Take me," with an edge to his voice. She extends her tongue,
leans forward slightly, inhales deeply as he fills her mouth with
his cock. At first, he holds himself there in the silky warmth of
her mouth, her jaw aching as it accommodates his girth. Then
he grips her head with both hands and rocks his hips, slowly
fucking her mouth the same way he fucks her cunt or her ass or
her tits, as Veronica rakes her fingernails along the undersides of
Vince's ass and down the backs of his thighs.

Veronica likes the reminder that the life of her own comes
with strings attached. She gags around his cock at first, but then
her throat muscles relax and she allows herself to surrender, to
let herself be used. She curls her tongue along the underside of
Vince's cock, enjoying the texture of him. After Vince comes, he
casts his eyes downward. Veronica straddles his feet and lowers
herself until her pussy grazes the leather of her husband's shoes.
She wraps her arms around his legs, and sighs as Vince rests a
gentle hand atop her head. She starts sliding back and forth,
her pussy getting wetter, her clit slick and throbbing. The closer
she gets to coming, the faster and harder she grinds. Her thigh
muscles strain; they tremble. She is always sweaty, her clothes
clinging to her body as an orgasm rolls through her, radiating
out from her cunt to every end of her body. She kisses Vince's
shoes once more. She smells herself on him. After he leaves her

to the rest of her day, she gathers her composure and slips back into the life of her own.

Vince and Veronica met when he saw her as a patient in the emergency room. After setting the broken bone in her arm, he sat on the rolling stool next to the hospital bed where she rested and said, "I'd like to take you out sometime."

Veronica sat up and arched an eyebrow. "Isn't that against the rules?"

Vince smiled coldly. "I'd like to take you out sometime."

Veronica looked at her arm, freshly casted, and held it out. "Give me your number," she said.

Two weeks later, Vince took her to an Ethiopian restaurant. They ate *wat* with *injera* and drank wine. They talked about everything and nothing. Toward the end of the meal, without ceremony, Vince said, "I am a man with brutal appetites."

Veronica was quiet. She had known all kinds of men, many of them brutal. Vince was the first to acknowledge his desires so frankly. She eyed him carefully—his thick black hair, roughly chiseled features, cold blue eyes. She decided she could love this man who knew himself so well, stated what he wanted so shamelessly. She could give him exactly what he needed to satisfy his appetites. Veronica wrapped her fingers around the stem of her wineglass and raised it toward him. Vince nodded, and explained in explicit detail what he would take from her. As she listened, Veronica crossed her legs, squeezing her thighs together. An unfamiliar warmth raced across her cheeks and down her neck. Her chest tightened.

When he finished, Vince said, "I'm not looking for a maid. I'm not looking for a mother. I'm looking for a body. I also know how to appreciate that which I am allowed to take."

Veronica reached beneath the table for Vince's hand, pulled it between her thighs. As he slid two fingers inside her, she looked right into his eyes and said, "That's important."

On their wedding night, Vince told Veronica that he didn't believe in punishment. He believed in discipline. Then he taught her the difference. He had converted the spare bedroom of their home into a discipline chamber with a St. Andrew's cross, a leather-covered paddling bench, and a sling hanging in the far corner. The wooden floors gleamed and the room was well lit. On one wall, there was a wide range of toys, some of which Veronica recognized, and others with which she would soon become familiar. As Veronica slowly walked around the room, dragging her fingers along each piece of equipment, Vince said, "I'll never understand why so many people believe this sort of thing should be done in darkness."

Veronica nodded, then turned away from Vince, asking him to unzip her wedding dress. As she stepped out of the layers of silk and lace, she said, "I agree." Then she stood against the cross, lowering her head. Her entire body relaxed as Vince fastened leather cuffs around her wrists and ankles, kissing the backs of her thighs as he worked his way upward. For a long while, Vince stood behind his new wife, inhaling her scent, letting his hands memorize the contours of her body. He cupped a breast in each hand and squeezed roughly, watching her flesh splay between his fingers. After twisting her nipples until she winced, her body arching into the pain, he pinched her nipples between a pair of clamps, connected by a thin gold chain.

Veronica felt drowsy. Her head lolled to one side and she smiled. Vince stepped away, and she felt a rush of cold air in the separation between their bodies. She shivered. Vince smacked her ass, smiling as her skin rippled beneath his hand. A blush of red quickly appeared. He smacked Veronica's ass again, harder this time, his hand stinging as it rebounded. "Discipline," he said, "is a reminder." Veronica's entire body tensed. The room was silent save for the sound of Vince's shoes as he crossed the room and eyed his wall of toys, selecting a few. He set his implements on the floor next to Veronica's body and picked up a long stainless steel paddle, with three rows of holes. He dragged the paddle across her shoulders and Veronica shivered. Then he raised the paddle in the air and brought it down twice in rapid succession. A darker shade of red blushed across Veronica's ass. She flexed her feet. A bead of sweat trickled down her neck and along her spine.

Vince began to smack Veronica's ass with the paddle in a firm and steady rhythm. Veronica barely had time to breathe between each blow. She closed her eyes, forced herself to relax, to fall into the pain. The harder Vince paddled her ass, the freer she felt. Then he stopped and dropped the paddle to the ground. She gasped at the clatter it made. Vince picked up another toy. He perched his chin on her shoulder and said, "Close your eyes. Open your mouth." She obliged willingly and felt something wide and rubbery in her mouth. "Get it wet," Vince said. Veronica lathed the foreign object with her tongue until Vince was satisfied. Then he spread her asscheeks apart and slowly worked what she now realized was an anal plug into the tight fissure of her ass. She could feel her body resisting, but Vince's will was more resolute than that of her body. Her body stretched around the plug, and after a short while, the sharp throbbing dulled into a pleasant discomfort. She felt swollen, full.

Veronica felt her head being pulled back, the muscles of her neck stretched to their limit. Vince slid his other hand from between her breasts up her throat, and he squeezed as he pressed his lips against hers, shoving his tongue between her lips. They kissed almost violently and, overwhelmed by the very burn of her skin, Veronica moaned into Vince's mouth. She thought, *I would say* I do *all over again.* She opened her mouth wider, nipped Vince's lower lip between her teeth. He pulled away for a moment and said, "Yes. I like that. Don't ever back down from me." Veronica leaned in, wanting more of Vince's lips against hers. He tightened the grip of his fingers in her hair, holding her lips a breath away from his. He followed the sensuous arcs of each lip with the tip of his tongue. He whispered that she was his whore and she whispered back, "Yes. Yes I am." They kissed again, harder this time, so hard that they could feel the bone beneath the flesh of their lips. Vince flicked his tongue against hers a final time, then brought his lips to her shoulder, first licking the salt from her skin, then sinking his teeth into her body. Veronica hissed, again arching into the sharp pain.

Vince reached down for a new toy, draped it over her shoulder. Veronica moaned, louder this time, as she felt several long strands of leather draping down over her breasts. Vince kissed the small indentations left by his teeth and took a few steps back. With a flick of the wrist, he let the cat-o'-nine-tails dance across her back lightly, just enough to tease. Another flick of his wrist, and a second dance of the whip came, a slow one. Vince draped the whip over her shoulder again, this time pulling it toward him, letting the tails drag down Veronica's back. He pulled his arm back, and without warning, released a vicious blow. Her entire body strained upward. Veronica clenched and unclenched her fingers. Another blow landed. Then came a steady rain of leather against her skin, the expanse of her back turning pink, then red, then a darker shade of red.

Veronica felt each blow down through her bones. After what seemed like hours, a thin sheen of sweat covered her entire body. Vince could see the streaks of the whip's tails in the perspiration. He threw the whip against Veronica's body until he could raise his arm no more.

"Do you understand discipline?"

Veronica nodded limply. "Yes," she whispered hoarsely.

Vince dropped the whip, gently released his new wife from her bondage and carried her across the threshold of their bedroom. He laid her in the middle of their bed and knelt between her legs. As he removed the nipple clamps, setting them on the night table, she cried out and shuddered, the blood rushing back to the puckered, sensitive nubs.

Veronica looked up at Vince and saw unexpected kindness in his eyes. "Have I pleased you?" she asked.

Vince finished undressing, then crawled back into bed, lying on his side next to Veronica. He slid one hand down her flat stomach and between her thighs and started stroking Veronica's clit with his thumb as he slid two fingers inside her cunt where she was wet and waiting for him. He pressed her clit hard and Veronica raised her hips, wanting more. Tears welled in her eyes. "Have I pleased you?" she asked again, her voice stronger this time. Vince slid his wet fingers into his mouth and savored the taste of her. Then he covered her body with his, buried his cock deep in her cunt. Veronica spread her legs wide. She clenched around him and Vince took a deep breath, tried to control himself. Veronica's entire body expanded, opening to her husband in every way he needed. Her ass continued to throb and pucker around the plug. She felt consumed. She arched her back, pressing her breasts against Vince's chest, enjoying the firmness of his body against hers.

Vince clasped her throat again, squeezing harder this time. "Look at me," he said.

Veronica opened her eyes and held her husband's gaze. She met each thrust, urging him deeper. Beads of sweat from his face fell into her mouth and she swallowed, trying to memorize the taste of his body. As she crested a new wave of pleasure and her body began its familiar descent into bliss, she asked one final time, "Have I pleased you?"

Vince reared back, holding the tip of his cock at the sensitive, quivering inner lips of her cunt. He squeezed Veronica's throat harder, and she wrapped one hand around his wrist. Vince thrust forward. Veronica cried out again, feeling a blade of pleasure so deeply, she thought her body might split at the heart. Vince kissed her chin, then her lips. The kiss was so soft it sent a frisson of pleasure curling around her spine. He stared at her for a moment longer. Finally, he said, "Yes."

THE NEGOTIATION

Remittance Girl

The dark mahogany boardroom table reflected sharp-edged inverted facsimiles of the two individuals who sat opposite each other. The flat dark lake faithfully mirrored the opponents while leaving an inky gulf between them.

The woman sat composed but rigid. The black hair smoothed to her head and bound in a chignon also reflected the streaks of light that shot into the room between the slats of the venetian blinds. Beneath the dark, arched brows, hazel eyes stared out calmly from behind her black-rimmed spectacles. But the edges of her scarlet lips twitched with tension, betraying the serenity of her other features.

She looked down and casually tugged at the cuff of her understated suit jacket. This would have gone unnoticed but for the fact that she wore no shirt beneath it. The jacket buttoned snugly at her waist, parting above to reveal the cleft of her perfect breasts. Beneath the table, and beneath her short wool skirt, she crossed a pair of stocking-sheathed legs. The friction whispered as one nylon thigh slid over the other. In the stillness of the room, it sounded like the sweep of a curtain.

"Your offer is insulting. It does not even begin to reflect the value of our assets. Surely you will admit that we possess something you need. Therefore, the offer needs to be compatible with the level of that need. If this was the opening gambit, sir, it has failed."

The man across the table leaned back into the concave comfort of the black leather seat. With his back to the window, the sharp lines of his jaw, nose and brow were accentuated by shadows. They rendered his expression inscrutable. He inhaled deeply and laced his fingers together, resting them on his stomach. He wore a somber suit to match hers, but a white shirt nestled like frost between the lapels of his open jacket; the burgundy tie, a dark red river against the snow. His gaze swept the broad expanse of the polished wood, resting momentarily on the inverted image that pooled like liquid before his opponent.

"The offer reflects nothing more than market forces and the risks inherent in a merger of this type. When two corporate entities of equal size merge, the likelihood of short-term instability is great. We need to account for this. Furthermore, we are negotiating in good faith. Many of your assets are, as yet, unevaluated."

The woman considered a moment and then placed both hands on the lip of the table and pushed. Her chair rolled back, away from the table, affording her opponent a head-to-toe view of her.

"In the interests of full disclosure, we are willing to allow an assessment to take place," she said cordially. "Let it never be said that these negotiations were tainted in any way by subterfuge or deception."

Slowly, she uncrossed her legs and parted them until the hem of her short skirt pulled taut against her thighs. Each glossy black stiletto settled firmly into the plush gray carpeting. Then, calmly, she shifted in her seat, sliding her hips forward. The friction of wool against leather caused her skirt to ride up and exposed twin bands of creamy skin above the dark lines of her sheer black stay-ups.

Her opponent leaned forward, resting his forearms on the table. His eyes fixed on the dark space between her parted thighs. He inhaled deeply again and then, suddenly, pushing his own chair back, stood up. He walked slowly beside the long line of empty chairs around the table and stopped beside one, on her side. He pulled it out, turned it sideways and sat down.

"I always find that face-to-face negotiations are more productive," he whispered, reaching over, laying his hand on the arm of her chair and swiveling it. The woman allowed her heels to drag deep furrows through the carpet's weave as the chair rotated. Once again they were eye to eye, only much closer now, and without the barrier of the table between them.

She surveyed her opponent carefully. Out of the shadow, she could see just how angular his face was. Patrician, and slightly arrogant, his smile rose but did not quite take in the steel gray eyes beneath the heavy salt-and-pepper brows. His aquiline nose still cast a dark shadow across his left cheek, and she could see that his slicked-back hair was shot through with silver.

This was disconcerting. She had thought her opponent perhaps a year or two older than her. But realizing that he was many years her senior, she feared his experience might very well slant the negotiations in his favor. However, as she resumed her position, she noticed that his gaze had dropped to the void between her legs and that, almost imperceptibly, a small muscle on the side of his jaw twitched.

The woman sighed softly and edged her hips even farther forward in the chair. The leather squeaked softly as the underside of her thighs slid over it. She smiled, one corner of her mouth lifting slightly higher than the other.

"As you can see, the assets are as listed and as described," she said. "We are extremely proud of who we are. And, as I said before, your offer does not reflect the quality of our corporate structure. Furthermore, ours are not the only assets that require valuation. It would be imprudent of us not to assure ourselves that our partner in this merger possessed properties of equal or greater value."

The man had himself slid down slightly in his seat and was apparently mesmerized by what was now on display before him. In fact, the prominent bulge in his trousers seemed to suggest that a better offer was to be expected shortly. An elbow on each armrest, he steepled his hands and touched his fingers to pursed lips. After a considerable period of consideration, he exhaled and looked her in the eye.

"You realize that a merger is not the only option for us? A buyout would suit us just as well. In fact, after careful thought, a simple buyout might be the most profitable move for us. It would provide for a far more reliable corporate governance structure. There would be no doubt as to who was in charge."

The smile that had played on the woman's lips grew broader. But it wasn't acceptance; it was a challenge. The painted nails of her hand reached to the single button that held her suit jacket closed and undid it. Released, the lapels sprung apart to reveal pert, ivory globes, each the size of a small grapefruit. Modest coffee-colored areolas surrounded each dark pink nipple.

"A buyout is not completely out of the question," she said, her nipples stiffening in the cold office air. "But we certainly would not sell without verifying that the newly formed entity would have competent leadership. As a responsible corporation, we would need to know that our assets were being left in strong, responsible hands."

Her opponent leaned forward once again. This time, he placed a broad, well-manicured hand on each of her knees. He pulled gently and her chair rolled easily toward him. Sliding a firm hand along each thigh until they rested on bare skin, he let his thumbs glance slowly over the warm, tender skin between. Then farther, under the gray wool skirt, his hands roamed and then stopped, hidden from view.

She could hear his breath now, deeper and more urgent. She swallowed against the dryness in her mouth as his thumbs slid over her neatly trimmed mound. It was difficult to fight the desire to move her hips but she was sure that any sign of overeagerness on her part would weaken her side in the negotiations. Staring straight into his eyes, she cemented the placid expression on her face and calmed her own breathing. Casually she let her gaze slip down to his lap. The modest bulge that had been there previously had taken on far greater proportions, and his cock was clearly straining against the fabric of his trousers.

Just then, the two thumbs buried between her legs plunged between her labia, spreading them wide and exposing the pent-up wetness inside. Dexterously her opponent grazed the pad of one thumb over her throbbing clit. He moved the other one down and drew small persuasive circles around the entrance to her hole, tightening the circle each time until finally he pushed into her shallowly.

She licked furtively at her dry lips. If she allowed things to go on like this, there would be nothing left for her to bargain with. The woman took a deep, stuttered breath and, easing her stockinged foot free of its shiny stiletto, she raised a slender leg and nestled her sheathed foot in his lap. She moved her leg, using her toes to stroke the long, clearly delineated line of his erection. At first, she trailed over it lightly and felt it jump and strain, but then, noticing the beneficial results of her endeavors, she pressed more firmly, dragging the ball of her foot up and down the pulsing, covered shaft.

Her change of position had dislodged one hand. He did not fight her for territory, but ceded and improvised. Nonchalantly, he unbuttoned his trousers and slid his zipper down. Then, taking a firm grasp of her questing foot, he directed it inside his clothing and onto the hot, hard cock beneath.

His leadership was masterful indeed, she thought, feeling a spot of moisture soak into the nylon toe of her stocking. She pointed the toe and tickled gently but insistently at the sensitive area beneath the crown of his cock. Her opponent groaned and pressed his thumb deeper into her wet passage. For a moment, she actually wondered whether she hadn't gotten the upper hand but, in a serious breach of unity, her hips began to tilt and rock of their own accord, giving him deeper access and exposing her need.

Just then, as she had concluded that a buyout was by far the best offer, he pushed his chair back and stood up. Without a moment's warning, he lifted and pushed her, facedown, onto the boardroom table. Stepping swiftly behind her, he wrenched her skirt up over her hips. She felt the chilled air on her naked buttocks and the cool smooth wood beneath her breasts.

His hands stroked the silky skin of her ass proprietarily and his breath came ragged and noisy as he nudged her legs apart with his knees.

"I think we have moved past the initial stage of the negotiations," he panted. Between her legs, the woman felt the hot, sticky head of her opponent's cock; he snuggled the tip deep into the furrow of her cunt and teased it back and forth tantalizingly.

"This isn't a buyout, is it?" she panted hoarsely, struggling beneath him. All her strategies, all her carefully laid plans had come to naught. Her position was untenable, her gambit lost.

"No," her opponent grunted, pushing his thick pulsing cock into the tight wet velvet cave. "This, my dear," he gasped, thrusting in deep and holding himself there, buried to the hilt, "is a hostile takeover."

Still impaled, she felt him pull her jacket off and run his hands along the bare flesh of her back. How was she going to face her board? How would she explain the total change of ownership? How could she resist the delicious cock that, at this very moment, grew harder and thicker inside her? The woman whimpered her frustration and used her cunt muscles to beg for more, squeezing, milking him.

Her owner laughed gruffly and bent over her. His gold tie-clip pinched as he pressed his chest to her back and whispered into her ear. "Oh, what a greedy little cunt you have, my dear."

The moan escaping her throat was cut short as he pulled out fast and rammed his cock back into her hard. The force of the thrust shoved her over the gleaming surface, her moist skin tugging and stretching painfully beneath her. Half expecting the rest of the meeting to continue at this pitch, she was surprised when he leant forward again. "This is my company, and we do things my way, here," he said.

Filled with his cock, she felt him slowly grind into her over and over, his hips moving in a circular fashion as he stirred deep into her core. His hands reached beneath her to cup her tits, squeezing and tugging as he fucked.

She closed her eyes and reveled in the pleasure, spreading her legs as far apart as they would go. Deep inside, his cockhead pushed and pushed against her cervix, sending gorgeous rivers of electricity up her spine. Slowly, his thrusts became wilder, more urgent.

"Ahh, yes," he hissed. "Now...now, you're mine."

"Yes," she moaned, her orgasm building, coming closer with each stroke of his thick cock. "But...why...why didn't you just get the lawyers to do it? You could have bought a much stronger concern than ours."

He fucked her hard now, holding her hips as he plunged into her sweet hole repeatedly. She couldn't hold back any longer, crying out as she began to shudder and convulse. Brilliant floods of pleasure swept over her body, blossoming out and then narrowing down to a tight ring around his bursting prick.

Suddenly, he grunted and jerked, hot thick streams of cum pumping into her twitching cunt. She groaned as she felt the heat spread through her and clamped tight around him, begging him for more.

Collapsing down on her, burying his face in her neck, he whispered, "But I liked you so much, I bought the company."

A NIGHT AT THE OPERA

Evan Mora

I'm waiting for you.

I'm seated facing the entrance to the restaurant, at a choice and intimate table of your liking. I slowly swirl the contents of my glass—something subtle and red, uncorked and awaiting my arrival, a vintage of your choosing. It changes with each sampling—elegant, mysterious and complex, with a subtle but unmistakable intensity. I am reminded of you.

I sit with an air of casual disinterest in my surroundings, outwardly poised and relaxed. Nothing in my demeanor betrays the nervousness I feel as I await your arrival, save for a slight tremor in my hand as I raise my glass to my lips. I am dressed as you asked, in a simple sleeveless black dress, a favorite of yours.

The door opens and you cross the threshold, your gaze immediately and unerringly finding mine. My heart skips a beat, then resumes at an erratic, accelerated pace. One corner of your sensuous mouth curls slightly upward—I am revealed. I set down my glass and fold my hands in my lap, lowering my gaze. Your effect on me is profound, even at a distance. My body tightens with awareness and anticipation, as though awakened by your presence.

I raise my eyes to meet yours again—they've not left my face; I had not expected that they would. I drink in your appearance: your perfectly tailored gray suit with only the top button casually fastened, your black dress shirt accentuating your short dark hair and brilliant blue eyes. The hostess has engaged you in conversation, your body is inclined slightly toward her, and you answer her inquiries in your calm, self-assured way, your gaze still firmly holding my own. And then you move, slowly crossing the distance that separates us with lithe, confident strides. I am held captive by the strength in your frame; your body moves with the fluid grace and power of a jaguar stalking its prey.

You sit opposite me, and though my body yearns for your touch—your lips pressed to my cheek, a casual hand on my shoulder, a simple stroke of your finger on the inside of my wrist—you do not touch me, and my body struggles in desire and disappointment. My discomfiture pleases you, and you do nothing to alleviate it. Instead, you skillfully guide the conversation through appetizers, dinner and the bottle of wine, coaxing detailed and thoughtful responses from me despite the simmering arousal in my body that refuses to abate. You are fiercely intelligent and demand no less than my complete engagement in this as in all areas. You challenge me—and I am as seduced by the intensity of our debate as I am by the heat of your gaze and the promise of what is to come.

I am distracted by the sensual movement of your thumb stroking the curve of your wineglass. I can't look away, watching the pad of your thumb move in small lazy circles on the smooth surface of the glass. You ask me a question, but I'm

rendered incapable of speech, transfixed by the hypnotic movement of your hand. My body swells and responds as though it is
me you are caressing, as though it is my flesh you are exploring
and not some inanimate vessel. I close my eyes for a heartbeat
as a wave of intense longing floods through me. I am helpless,
trembling at the mere suggestion of your touch. When I meet
your eyes, I see the knowledge of your power over me reflected
in their depths, and I am stripped, as surely as if I were standing
naked before you.

We are headed to the theater, so I excuse myself to the restroom for a moment, in hopes of regaining a measure of control
over my arousal. I brace my hands on the edge of the sink, head
lowered, drawing deep calming breaths. But my respite is short
lived. I hear the barely perceptible sound of the door swinging
open and look up into the mirror to find you slowly advancing
toward me. I move as though to turn toward you, but you stop
me with a shake of your head. My back is to you, our gazes
locked in the mirror, and you halt your advance only when your
body is a hairsbreadth away from my own, your heat mingling
with mine.

Still, you don't touch me.

You lean forward, placing one hand immediately in front of
my own on the edge of the sink, your mouth—your beautiful
sensuous mouth—next to my ear. You tell me to take off my
panties, and I gasp at the intimacy of your command. I hesitate
for only a fraction of a second, but I know it's too long, and
your hand moves with decisiveness from the sink to the back
of my neck, and I am slowly bent forward at your insistence,
moaning now from the combined pleasure of your touch and
the vulnerability of my position. With your other hand, you
reach beneath my dress, fingers splayed, palm sliding up the
inside of my thigh until you reach my wetness. I am drenched

with my desire, and whisper only "Please," but I am denied even now, and your knuckles only glance over my flesh as your fingers wrap around the fabric of my thong and tear it off with a firm jerk of your hand.

My body trembles in the wake of your controlled aggression. You relinquish your hold on my neck, your hand slowly descending, tracing the curve of my spine, moving outward until it rests lightly against my hip. I feel you then—for one brief, almost imagined moment, I feel you—feel the reflexive tightening of your grip in the same instant that I feel your hips rock forward, the thick length of your cock unmistakable against my ass. I close my eyes, drowning in the sensation of you pressed so tightly against me...but just as quickly, you're gone. My eyes snap open and I cry out at the loss of your touch, but you are already moving to the door, holding it open and waiting for me to precede you out of the restroom, tucking my ripped panties into your suit jacket. I search your face for evidence of your desire, for some small sign that lets me know you are as affected by this exchange as I am, but your composure is intact, your face a mask that gives no emotion away.

We leave the restaurant, walking the short distance to the theater in silence, yours contemplative, mine tormented. I am awash with arousal, miserable with desire for you, and my body is proclaiming its need of you with wet, aching clarity. I am acutely aware that my sex is exposed beneath the thin veneer of my dress; the cool evening breeze kisses the moisture that has accumulated there and my cheeks flood with shame. I feel your knowing stare and struggle to regain my composure, but I can't. I know that if you were to lead me down any of the shadowed alleys we are passing and push me to my knees, your hand knotted in my hair, pressing my face to the front of your suit pants, I would eagerly use lips and teeth and tongue to free your cock and greedily swallow the length of it. I would work your cock until I gagged, until every inch of you was wet with my saliva, until your breathing grew ragged and your hips jerked convulsively and you threw your head back with the force of the orgasm tearing through your body. I would beg you to let me touch myself; I'd stroke my clit for you right there—on my knees, on the pavement in that shadowed alley until my cunt clenched and my clit exploded and I cried out my pleasure for you.

But you don't lead me down any alleys...you remain collected, smooth, and utterly in control.

Tosca is superb, but right now I hate Puccini. I hate the seconds and minutes and hours that stretch between this dark theater and lying naked beneath you. I hate that I think these thoughts, squirming quietly in my seat, when you are so clearly enjoying the performance. I feel like I am somehow letting you down because I can't rise above this driving need pulsing through my body. I worry my hands distractedly in my lap, unable to keep them folded demurely as I should.

I gasp with surprise at the feel of your hand on my thigh and am immediately stilled by its solid pressure. Though I can't make out the nuances of your expression, I feel your gaze locked on mine and feel a moment of quiet comfort—there is a measure of ease to be found in knowing that the play of emotions and wants coursing through my body is directed by you, like the maestro with his orchestra below.

With aching slowness, your hand traces invisible patterns across the top of my thigh. I scarcely breathe for fear that you will stop and am rewarded for my stillness when your hand dips lower, to the sensitive flesh of my inner thigh. The sound of the opera recedes, and my world narrows to the feel of you stroking me, inching closer to my wetness. Still, you keep me off balance, refusing to settle into a predictable rhythm; you stroke me and then pause, and I can do naught but tremble and hold my breath until you resume. Your fingers linger teasingly at the edge of my skirt until I bite my lip to keep from moaning aloud in supplication. Then, with a sinfully slow slide, they ease beneath the material and continue ever higher, until you are stroking my cunt, spreading my folds and taking possession of the wetness that meets you. My thighs spread farther apart of their own accord; this is my offering to you, this hot flood of arousal. Here in this confined space where I am stripped of words and actions to show you how I feel, it is all I have to offer. It is yours—it belongs to you, as surely as I do.

I know you approve because the heel of your hand clamps down on my pubic bone and your fingers penetrate my cunt so that you're gripping me firmly, my slick sex held tightly in your palm. You lean into me and whisper that I'm going to come for you, right here in the middle of the theater, sitting perfectly still, and without making a sound. Your voice is like sex to me; I feel each word you breathe into my ear across my clit, so wet for you that it drools off your knuckles and trickles between the cheeks of my ass. I nearly come from your words alone and nod my head, though really, it's not a question of agreeing. You slide your fingers out of my cunt and up to my clit, all teasing gone, demanding my orgasm with hard strokes, and then I'm coming in waves, cunt heaving as pleasure wracks my body. A second rush begins to coil in my belly but you stop your movement and say, "Enough," and I gasp, halted immediately on the edge of that precipice and robbed of breath, the pain it produces as acute and intense as the pleasure that hammered through me moments ago.

You wait until the sensation subsides, then remove your hand, wiping it clean with a handkerchief produced from your pocket. I feel dizzy and disoriented, and the final moments of the opera pass in a blur of music and applause, bright lights, the buzz of conversation sliding past me. I am aware of only the firm pressure of your hand in the small of my back, guiding me through the noise and into the quiet of your car, and of the constant thrum of my arousal as you guide us skillfully through the night, your beautiful square jaw thrown into profile by the passing headlights of oncoming traffic.

You don't touch me again until the door of your penthouse clicks shut behind us and you push me to the ground, one hand opening your fly even as your other reaches in to free your dick. I scramble to my knees as you grab the back of my head and then your cock is filling my mouth. I grab on to your legs to steady myself as you bury yourself in my throat with a rough thrust and I feel myself choke on your thick length, tears filling my eyes. I am filled with bliss, so wet I'm running down my thigh, thrilled at last to be able to touch you, to be used by you, to please you. You fuck my mouth and I struggle to take you in with some measure of grace but I cannot, and feel myself sinking into sensation: The feel of your suit pants beneath my fingertips. The wet slide of your cock over my lips. The feel of your hands knotted in my hair, pulling my head toward you in time with the rhythm you drive out with your hips. Your smell, a heady combination of cologne and arousal assaulting my senses. The silence, broken only by the shallow erratic sound of my breathing.

I want you to come. I want to feel you unravel and lose control. I want to feel the tremor in your thighs, feel your hands tightening in my hair. I want to show you how good I am for you. But you have other ideas. You relinquish your hold on me and take a step back, robbing me of your warmth and support and I falter, kneeling awkwardly before you, eyes downcast.

"Look at me," you say, and I do. I watch you release the button on your jacket and shrug it off, then toss it to a chair by the door. You remove your cufflinks, then your watch, placing them on the console table. You roll your sleeves up to mid-forearm, then unbutton your black oxford and leave it hanging open, lying in contrast to the white tank top revealed beneath. I drink in your appearance hungrily: your dark hair falling casually across your forehead, the slight flush staining your cheeks, your hard chest and taut stomach outlined by your tight white tank. I watch as one hand descends, wraps around your cock. I watch you stroke yourself, your cock still wet with my saliva. You are wildly beautiful, and I want you more than my next breath.

You tell me to get up, and with slow deliberation you close the gap separating us until I can feel your hot breath on my cheek and I need to look up to meet your eyes. You keep inching forward until I have no choice but to take a step back, and then another, until I'm up against the door with nowhere left to go. You ask me if I enjoyed dinner. I tell you I did. You ask me if I enjoyed the opera. I say yes. You shake your head, eyes glittering dangerously—I know better than to lie to you, you say. You pull my dress up until it's bunched around my hips, and your fingers find me again, thrusting deep into my slick hole, your eyes never leaving mine as I gasp with pleasure. You press your body against mine, still inside me, fucking me with a hard, even rhythm, telling me how you watched me squirm in my seat, how you smelled my arousal, like some bitch in heat. "Isn't that right?" you say, and I nod my agreement—I am whatever you tell me I am.

"You want my cock, hungry bitch?" You growl in my ear. I whimper and close my eyes, drunk on the heady combination of your words and the feel of your fingers pumping my cunt. But then you slap my face and I cry out, jolted back to the moment, mind racing, trying to figure out what I've done to displease you. "I asked you a question," you say. "Don't make me repeat myself." And I trip over myself in my eagerness to be redeemed, nodding my head, mewing my assent, telling you in a halting, breathy voice I barely recognize as my own how much I want your cock inside me, how starved I am for it. I beg you to fuck me and feel my cheeks flood with heat. I am the greedy whore you name me, my hungry cunt aching for release, and all the while you finger-fuck me, grinding into me up against the door.

I am rewarded for my answer with a kiss, and for the first time tonight I feel the sublime touch of your lips against mine, your tongue teasing the corners of my mouth, then aggressively demanding entry. I moan and eagerly yield to the pressure of your kiss, hands snaking up your chest to delve into the soft hair at the nape of your neck, reveling in the feel of your tongue stroking wetly against my own. You kiss me hungrily, dominating my mouth with ruthless intensity, the heat between us rising white hot.

You grip me by the waist, never breaking the kiss, and lift me up, my back still pressed against the door. I wrap my legs around your waist and you lean into me hard, moving one hand beneath me to bring yourself into position, and then I feel the thick head of your cock probing the mouth of my cunt, finding no resistance and then filling me, inch by agonizing inch. Hands beneath my thighs, your hips thrust slowly forward as you lower me more fully onto you, until I am filled to overflowing with you, breaking the kiss with a gasp as my body stretches to take you in. You smile then, the corner of your mouth moving upward with that same slow seductive curve you flashed in the restaurant. "Is that what you want?" you ask me, rocking forward again.

"Yes!" I hiss, and I feel you deep inside of me, feel you fucking me at last, feel your hips grinding into me, driving out the rhythm my body's been craving all night. There is no teasing in this now. You are strength and force and raw sex, giving me all that I can take, fucking me hard and fast, hips pistoning into me, growling that you want my orgasm, you want to feel my slobbering cunt clench around your dick, you want to feel my nails digging into you, hear me grunting, taste the sweat on my skin. I feel the tension rising in my body, feel it coiling tighter in my belly with every rough thrust and moist word you breathe. My thighs clamp around your waist even tighter, wanting more of you, ravenous for you even as you fuck me with a roughness that borders on violence. I know I'll hurt tomorrow, feel that sweet ache in my cunt that reminds me of this, of you. I moan with pleasure at the thought, and grab on to you all the harder, working my cunt feverishly on your cock in time with your raw thrusts until orgasm tears through my body and I cry out my release. You keep fucking me, never slowing your rhythm as spasms of pleasure rock through my cunt, and one wave of pleasure spills into the next until I think I can't possibly take any more.

Only then do you stop, lowering me spent and exhausted to the ground. I want nothing more than to curl into you and rest, but there's no respite for the wicked. You turn me over so that I'm on my knees in front of you, shoulders on the ground. You kneel behind me, one hand on my ass, the other guiding your slick cock into my aching cunt until I am impaled on your thick length. I can't help but moan at the feel of you filling me, and again as you start to move with slow thrusts, pulling back until only the head of your cock is in me, then pushing forward again, feeding me your cock inch by agonizing inch. You tell me to stroke my clit for you and I whimper a little, my flesh overly sensitive to the touch, but I obey you, circling the engorged tissue with light strokes. You tell me you want me to stroke myself for you like that until I come again, and I know a moment's misery because I don't honestly think I can. You slap my ass hard and I cry out. "Do it," you say, punctuating your words with hard thrusts.

It's easier somehow like that, with your cock driving into me aggressively, your hands gripping my hips tightly. I'll have bruises there too, evidence of your possession. I like your marks on me; I feel less naked in my nakedness with them. You moan then, and your fingers tighten reflexively on my hips, the speed of your thrusts increasing. Some primal feeling breathes new life into my sex, and I press my fingers more firmly into my clit, feeling it pulse, feeling that delicious tension start to rise again in time with your arousal. I hear your breathing, shallow and erratic, feel the tremor in your hands as your pleasure mounts, and stroke my clit harder, feeling my own pleasure rising in turn. I am undone by the feel of you coming apart, losing control as you pump your cock into me, as hard and fast as you can, until I hear you cry out your own release and my orgasm hits me like a freight train.

We collapse in a heap of tangled limbs and rumpled clothes and lie quietly until our hearts slow and our breathing calms and the cool air chills the sweat on our heated skin. You stand, offering me your hand, and lead me to your bed without a word. With gentle fingers and soft kisses, you remove my clothes, and then your own, pulling back the coverlet and sliding in beside me, urging my head onto your shoulder and covering us in a warm cocoon of blankets. You kiss my forehead tenderly and whisper that I am a good girl, that I am your girl. My heart soars. I belong to you.

MOMMY'S BOY

Doug Harrison

Marc had leaned his butt against the bondage bench, elbows resting on its leather surface. His sweaty torso was still heaving from his exertions. His condom-covered cock jutted in front of him. I couldn't help staring before I sidled over. I fantasized that he was a client, and I could imagine the excitement I would feel while securing him to the table—tightly, no movement possible. Not with an intricate rope harness, my specialty, but with wrist and ankle restraints, spread-eagled, his taut muscles stretched to their limit as they pushed against his smooth skin, accentuating his gorgeous physique. I could slide my tongue and fingers over every inch of his body, fuck his mouth with my tongue, tease his cock until he screamed for release, and lower myself ever so slowly onto its hardness and fuck us into oblivion.

I cleared my mind and perched next to him, feet jutting over the edge, and despite my age, must have looked the picture of a schoolgirl sitting on a playground table. I put my hand on his thigh. A few minutes passed, during which Marc stared vacantly at the far wall while his hard-on wilted.

"Looks like it went well," I said.

"I hope so," Marc replied.

"How do you feel?"

"Okay, I guess. A little winded, but that will pass. Felt strange at first, getting paid to do something as natural as S/M."

"I've learned to trust my instincts."

"That's what I did," Marc said reflectively. He stood, stretched, and removed the condom. He glanced in one of the full-length mirrors as he tossed the well-filled rubber into a wastebasket.

"Yeah, yeah, you're beautiful." I smirked. "Not bad for a guy who just turned thirty-five," I added. "And *our* client thinks so, too. He seemed...how should I say it? Serene but pensive. Whatever you did, it worked. He wants to know when he can see you again. It's that old magic."

"I'm glad," Marc grinned. "Glad I could assist 'Mistress Michelle.' Besides, I enjoyed myself."

"As soon as he stammered that he 'wanted to be with a man,' I thought of you."

"It's good I was back in the area."

"Yes, as I mentioned on the phone, I heard through the grapevine that you'd returned."

"The S/M community has big ears."

"And even larger mouths."

We both laughed.

"What brought you back?" I asked.

"We engineers move around. But it's good to be here in Silicon Valley. More perversion than in a Midwestern town, even a large one."

"And more acceptance."

"You got it."

"I remember seeing you at the Janus play party years ago," I said.

"My first one."

"Obviously. You looked, well, unsettled, but your commanding presence overrode that."

"And you showed me the ropes, so to speak."

Again we laughed.

"And you learned quickly," I said. "Made quite a reputation in the community." I winked. "With both the ladies and the men."

"Yep."

"Which do you prefer?"

"Hard to say, I mean, difficult to say. Fifteen years of marriage and two kids leave an impression."

"I watched you meander from pansexual parties to gay sex clubs."

"Yeah, and a boyfriend or two."

I shrugged. "Well, you're here now. I hope you haven't lost your touch with the women."

"Hell, no! I'm still footloose and fancy free." Mark was too proud to blush, but his eyes sparkled. "It's great to be here. Thanks for inviting me."

"Thank you! Our time together, even with a client, made me think of how much I've missed you. God, even if I had to pay for your sexy body, I'd gladly do it." I languidly traced one well-manicured nail across Marc's sharply defined pecs.

"For you, it's always free," Marc shot back.

I paused almost imperceptibly, and whispered in soft, husky tones, "Take me down, Marc, take me down."

Marc cocked his head and raised one eyebrow. "No limits?"

"No limits, baby." I threw my hair back with a quick flick of my head to disguise any nervousness, real or perceived.

Marc covered the short distance between us in two quick strides, his cock hardening in the process. He grabbed my red hair and hauled me to his height. He scanned my few silver locks and glared directly into my eyes. "You really want it, don't you, crone?"

I flinched. Mark clearly knew the honorific used by myself and my friends, and his pejorative manner cut me to the quick. Well, I had asked for it.

"Lick my boots." Marc dropped, almost threw me to the carpet. "Let me feel your mommy tongue through the leather. Make love to your boy's boots."

I captured Marc's right boot with a firm, two-handed grip. I pressed my face tightly to the toe box and quickly covered it with kisses. I licked, and dug my teeth into the black, shimmering leather. Marc put his left foot on my shoulder.

"Goddamn, you're a terrific footrest," he hissed.

"Ooh, yes, yes," I moaned. I glanced up at Marc and felt the lines around my eyes soften in the dim light.

"Shut up and keep licking," Marc said while he kicked my derriere with the side of his boot. I returned to my task with renewed vigor after his remark about the firmness of my well-rounded ass. Although I'm confident in the appeal of my body, at age fifty-one, every compliment helps.

"That's it, make your boy's feet feel real good," Marc encouraged. "I like you on your knees. That's where you belong, slut. Feels good down there, doesn't it?"

I nodded.

"Now the other one. Make the other one feel good, too."

I switched feet. Marc reached into his vest pocket. I snuck a quick look. He pulled out a pair of gloves and methodically donned them behind his back.

"You're pretty good at licking boots, slut," he snarled. He

yanked me to a kneeling position. "Look, here's a present for Mommy." I inhaled deeply while Marc drew the back of his hand under my nose. The leather glove was skintight and lead weights were sewn into the knuckles.

He stuck his thumb into my mouth. I shuddered and sucked on it. My hesitation morphed into greed. Marc cupped my jaw in his hands and stared into my eyes.

"I love the surprise in your eyes." A firm slap landed on my left cheek. "I like to see fear in your eyes—it turns me on." He smacked my other cheek. "I'm going to give you pain." *Slap.* "I know you like it—it turns you on, too." *Slap. Slap.* "I'm going to give you so much pain you can't take any more…" *Slap.* "But you'll want more." *Slap.* "Just like the pain pig you are." *Slap. Slap. Slap.* "I'll have you begging for pain, not knowing if it's you or someone else screaming."

Marc paused. "Got that, bitch?"

I whimpered, squirming in his tight grasp.

Marc pushed me to the floor. "Get out of those damn domme clothes," he ordered. "Hurry!"

I twisted and tugged to quickly remove boots, skirt and bustier. My eyes darted to my vibrator, dangling from a peg on the wall, cord tightly wound in a neat bundle. It was within easy reach.

"You don't need your fuckin' vibrator," Marc shouted. He sneered while I whimpered in embarrassment. "An old lady's best friend—do it with electricity—yeah, well, I'll show you a good enough time. Now crawl over to the horse; I'm gonna give you a real ride." He pushed me down on all fours, and urged me across the room with the tip of his boot.

I halted in front of the walnut sawhorse. Its top and legs were padded in black leather, and numerous metal rings were bolted along its perimeter.

"Get your ass up there," Marc commanded. I climbed onto the horse, butt hanging over the edge, my chin resting on the opposite end. Marc chose several leather straps from the collection arranged in coils on a shelf. He ran one of the thongs under my nose, pausing long enough for me to savor the familiar aroma. "When I'm finished, you're not going anywhere."

He secured my thighs, calves, and upper arms to the legs of the horse. I moaned with pleasure when he cinched each strip of leather. He finished by tightening a wide belt about my waist.

"You really like this, don't you, giving up all your goddamn power, surrendering to your boy?" Marc asked. I again nodded.

"Answer me, now!" he ordered. He stood in front of me and pulled my hair back until our eyes met.

I squealed through my tears.

Marc's dick was harder than it had been all day. Pulsing veins throbbed along the thick shaft.

"Then suck on this. Show me how much you like boy cock." Marc slapped my cheeks with his dick. I turned my head and finally grabbed the tip of his bobbing prick with pursed lips. Marc jammed it down my throat and I gasped for breath.

"You cocksucking bitch. That's it, make your boy feel real good. This is what you've been waiting for all night, isn't it? Take it, you slut, take it!"

I was a good cocksucker, even in this position, even with Marc's larger-than-average dick. I nibbled, I slurped, I sucked. Marc brushed my shoulders with his gloved hands, and worked up to a series of hard blows, each one landing when his dick reached the apex of his thrust.

"Yes, yes, yes," I gurgled in louder and louder tones, my fists clenched.

Suddenly Marc paused, and stood very still. "Wait." We remained motionless for about ten seconds. His dick softened somewhat. My eyes widened when I tasted the first few drops of acrid piss. My panting slowed and I sealed my lips tightly around his dickhead. I had traveled this route a few times, always for a fee, but never with such a stud.

"That's it. Don't spill a drop. Here it comes." Marc let go. He breathed deeply and grunted while he forced a steady stream into my mouth. I swallowed feverishly to keep up with the flow. I used my throat muscles, not moving my lips, a technique that only a good cocksucker could easily adapt.

"Good, very good," Marc said with a nod of approval. The flow slowly subsided. He removed his dick from my mouth and wiped off his piss slit with a few wisps of my hair.

I sighed.

Marc knelt and kissed me roughly on the lips and then walked to the wall. My eyes followed his every move. "Think I'll try some caning," he said in a mocking voice, throwing his gloves into the corner.

"No," I wailed. "I hate caning!"

"Quiet," Marc growled. He picked up a few canes and swished each one back and forth. "Haven't done much caning," he mumbled, making sure I could hear his ruminations. He chose a three-foot-long birch cane, about a quarter inch thick, and swaggered over to me, flexing the cane with every step. I shuddered.

"Stick that pretty mommy ass up in the air for your boy," he ordered. "As much as you can!" he added.

"Oh, shit," I grumbled while I complied.

"What's that?" Marc questioned. "Louder."

"Oh, shit," I bawled.

"That's what I thought you said. Here's something to make you shit." He landed a vicious swipe across my ass. I screamed.

"No, no, I'll be good, don't hit me again," I pleaded.

"You'll be what I say you'll be. Now shut up and take it."

Marc backed off and concentrated on my left cheek, hitting me lightly until I groaned. Then he changed hands and repeated the performance on my right side.

"Almost like flogging," he said. He grabbed a similar cane. "Now for some two-handed percussion."

He positioned himself directly behind me and simultaneously hit each cheek lightly. He slowly built to heavier blows, coaxing me to writhe while my yaps increased to howls.

"Take three good ones," he commanded and placed the canes on my ass, so I could feel where he was going to hit. "Here it comes," he yelled. I stared at his reflection in a full-length mirror as he raised both hands over his head. The canes landed with a loud whacking sound. I screamed. Marc pressed the canes into my flesh while the stinging subsided.

"Good-looking marks," Marc observed in a loud voice, while he repeated the stroke.

Tears formed in my eyes.

"Last one." *Whack!* My entire body spasmed. It was a long five seconds before I exhaled.

Marc rubbed his hand over several welts. "Nice, in fact, quite nice. Ready for more?"

"Oh, shit—I mean, yes."

Marc pummeled me with rapid blows of mixed intensity. I thrashed so much that the horse bounced back and forth and edged toward the wall.

"Do I have to chase you around the room, cunt?"

He pulled the bench away from the wall and turned it, despite the deep pile of the black carpet. He was strong, confirmed by his next whacks.

"Good," he soon observed. "You're finally bleeding for your boy." Marc's ferocity spiraled when my blood surfaced. Pain flowed from my butt into my entire body and consumed me. I was on fire, a heretic chained to a stake, praying for blessed oblivion. He finally backed off, and I floated with the rhythmic thudding of the canes. He ditched one cane and his blows subsided into nothingness while he stroked my back. At last he stopped. He paused, gave me a drink of water through a straw, and cleaned my butt with antiseptic wipes. "Nice pattern of cross-hatched welts back here," he announced.

Marc waited until my breathing settled into a slow rhythm and then knelt in front of my tear-streaked face and donned rubber gloves, finger by finger. He returned to his position at the rear of the horse. He paused until my anticipation and fear rose to mix in an unseen cloud between us. Then he reached under my hips and massaged my clit with the thumb and index finger of one hand, while rubbing my tender butt with his other hand. My breathing and squirming guided his ministrations as my excitement and arousal swelled.

"Oh, my god," I soon cried out. "Oh, I'm...I'm coming."

"Go for it," Marc yelled.

"Oh, fuck, fuck, fuck," I screamed. I raised my head and reared back the few inches my bondage would permit, let out one final yell, and collapsed into the leather.

Marc stepped back, all smiles. He knelt in front of me and cradled my head.

"How are you doing? Need anything?"

I hesitated as I tried to sort convoluted thoughts. "I'm...I'm doing fine. Sure not thirsty," I mumbled. "What next?" I asked tentatively.

Marc rolled on a condom and lubed his dick. He leaned onto my butt and rubbed his cock between my asscheeks. "Your little boy is going to fuck his mommy," he said softly.

"Oh," I muttered.

"In the butt," Marc continued.

I didn't move and remained silent. Marc lowered his torso and slithered along my back. "That's what you want, isn't it, Mommy, to be ass-fucked like a boy?" he teased in a soft whisper.

No answer.

"Tell me you want it," Marc cajoled in a louder voice.

Again no answer.

Marc stood and stuck his slippery finger up my asshole, none too gently.

"I want it. I want it!"

Marc pushed his dick into my hole, slowly, but didn't ease the pressure until he was all the way in. Then he plunged back and forth in a teasing corkscrew motion. "It's a turn-on looking at the red stripes on your butt while I'm ass-fucking you," he said. He pummeled my shoulders with both palms. I wheezed while the wind was knocked out of me. Marc whacked my ass.

"Fag hag, that's what Mommy is," Marc sneered. "Likes to get fucked in the ass by a fag. Straight boys aren't good enough for you." He grabbed my hips and pumped furiously. "Bet you can feel this hard dick on the back of your cunt."

I clenched my sphincter, but a few yellow drops trickled down the edge of the horse.

"So I'm fucking the piss out of you, huh," Marc said. "Go for it, Mommy, pee on your goddamn precious rug!"

"No, no, no," I protested, but I couldn't stop. Marc kept fucking me while piss gushed off the horse. Some of it ran down his chaps and onto his boots.

"Christ, on my chaps and boots!" Marc bellowed. He tugged his dick out, stomped to the other end of the horse and stood in front of me. "Lick these chaps clean, piss slob," he ordered. My tongue darted back and forth across his chaps while he positioned himself to make sure I captured every possible drop. "Now these boots again," he directed. He held each foot to my mouth, and I rapidly cleaned off the leather.

"An okay job," Marc conceded, strolling back to his original position. He slid his dick into my asshole and resumed his fucking.

"I'm going to pound that pussy of yours into the horse." Marc swung his hips back and forth in increasing arcs, forcing my pelvis to slide along the wet leather. I grabbed the front legs of the horse and began humping it in sync with Marc's lunges.

"Christ, I'm going to come," I howled.

"That's it, Mommy, come again for your boy. Don't need your vibrator now, do you?" Marc grabbed my shoulders, digging in his nails. "Think I'll join you—yeah, let's come together."

I shrieked in a quivering crescendo.

"I'm coming in you, I'm coming," Marc joined in. His final lunge sent the horse hopping, and he growled deeply while his dick spasmed. Then he flopped onto my back, his arms around me. Our gasps subsided and our breathing slowed and synchronized.

We rested a few more minutes, and Marc untied me. He led me to the wall, guided me to a reclining position and positioned my head in his lap. He stroked my hair.

I looked up at him. "Thanks, baby. You're the only one I can surrender to so completely." I rubbed my bottom. "I'll think of you every time I sit down for the next few days."

"Good." Marc smiled. "And your clients won't see the marks."

"I really needed that."

Mark kissed me on the forehead. "I could tell."

NO GOOD DEED

Alison Tyler

The click of the handcuffs resonated inside Jamie. No other sound in the world had the same effect. The lock shut with a cold, crisp finality, and she knew that the only way she'd be loose again was when Killian decided to set her free. From the stern expression on his face, Jamie knew that moment was a long way off.

"What's the name of the game?" Killian asked as he bound her slim ankles to the footboard. There was no expression in his voice: not anger, not disappointment. She wished that he would yell at her, call her names, do something to show that he wasn't simply moving on autopilot.

She turned her head to watch him over her shoulder, dark bangs fluttering in front of her eyes, so that she saw him through the wisps of her hair. Although she had an excuse to offer, she didn't say a word—didn't dare.

"Come on, baby."

But there it was. The "baby" that let her feel the emotion swell up inside of her, the way it had the very first time he'd called her that. She could remember the night clearly, as if she had black-and-white photographs of each separate moment in time. They'd met at a party. She'd shaken his hand at the start of the evening, thought he was attractive—tall and slim, an air of the rogue about his edges in spite of his expensive shirt, leather jacket—but she hadn't felt any reciprocation. Only later in the night, when she'd been talking to another man by the bar, had Killian come up behind her.

"Ready to go, baby?"

Like they were a couple. Intrigued, she'd followed his lead, slid on her coat, let him take her by the wrist. She'd been his ever since.

He'd led her to the car, pressed her up against the hood, got his mouth right close to her ear and whispered, "You flirting?"

The hot sensation of guilt flooded through her. Had she been? Well, yeah. But she'd come to the party a single. Single people could flirt. She tried to explain this to Killian, but the look in his eyes stopped her. Finally, stammering, she'd said, "Yes, I was."

"Honesty's always the best policy with me, kid," he said, nodding. "But that doesn't mean I'm not going to give you a spanking."

It was as if he'd gotten inside her head, seen all of her fantasies. No man had ever talked to her like that before.

"Do you understand?"

She nodded. She didn't really, though. What was he offering?

"If you get into that car with me, I am going to spank your ass until you cry. And then I'm going to take you home, cuff your wrists over your head, and lick your sweet pussy until you come like you've never come before. And the whole time I'm licking you, you're going to be imagining the spanking I'm going to give you after."

Jesus fucking Christ. Her knees felt weak. Even if this was only a one-night stand, even if she never saw him again, she knew she'd go with him. Thank god she'd worn pretty panties. That was the final rational, or at least semirational, thought she had as she let him position her over his lap in the backseat of the Chevy, felt his warm hand push her skirt to her waist, felt the stinging slap of the first blow through her hot-pink knickers.

Now, his voice remained flat. "What's the name?"

This was like some twisted version of *Rumpelstiltskin*. She felt a laugh welling up, and she bit the insides of her cheeks to keep the sound contained. Chuckling now would be a bad idea. Doing anything that Killian did not specifically request would be a bad idea. A shudder ran through her as he tightened the leather on her ankles. She was stretched taut, totally naked on the pale pink satin sheets, her thighs spread, her pussy pressed firmly to the mattress. She could feel the wetness under her, and her cheeks burned. Being turned on wasn't something she could control. If Killian tested her, if he slid his fingers between her nether lips, she was done for.

"The game is called *Punish the Slut*," Killian said as he walked around her. There was a dangerous tone in his voice now. "God, kid, you're such a good player, you should have known that. I mean, you're a fucking champion."

Was she? She felt like she was in the weeds.

He'd met her this evening at the bar at eight, just like they'd planned. She'd been perched up on the corner stool, talking to a handsome man, and when Killian walked in, the man placed a hand on her thigh, right below the hem of her skirt, on her bare skin.

Timing is everything.

Killian hadn't said a word. He'd slapped a twenty on the bar, gripped her wrist, and pulled her out of the place. There was no conversation in the car. Not a single threat or recrimination. He took her home, told her to strip, and bound her down to the bed.

That's where they were now.

She could have refused if she'd wanted to. She could have explained herself, gotten out of this mess with only a few easy sentences.

The thing was, she didn't want to.

Punish the Slut.

She knew the rules well enough, after all.

The blindfold slipped into place—black velvet, soft like feathers. The ball gag was next. She thrashed as he buckled the hated gag; she couldn't help herself. The taste of the rubber was far too unpleasant to take willingly. Bitter, but reminiscent of some faraway memory—like black tar and licorice. Killian seemed to like her struggles, easily exerting the force to keep her steady as he fastened the gag tight.

What was coming next made her heart race and her clit throb. He was going to cane her. If she had wanted him to go easy on her, if she'd wanted him to let her off with a warning, she'd lost the chance to say—to beg, to explain.

The gag was fastened. There wasn't even a chance for a safeword. With Killian, she'd never needed one before; no reason to think she would now.

On most days, the cane stood in the corner of their closet, leaning against the wall. He hardly ever used it. They hardly ever reached this point. But she'd been craving the pain, jonesing for it, like any addict—like any hungry little needling.

But that didn't make this any easier.

Pain is pain, whether you want it or not; whether it soothes your soul, calms your needs, smoothes out the roughness of your edges. Pain is still fucking pain.

rt="108"108108108108108108108108108108108108108108108108108108108108108108108108108108108108 108108

He let her feel the cane before the first stroke. He set the length of the weapon against her naked ass, rested the weight on her. She was lost in sensory deprivation. There was no way to speak, no chance to see the look in his eyes when he cut into her. She had no idea how many strokes he was going to land—no clue when he would start or when he would end. That made the fear rise up strong inside the pit of her belly.

She could hear him walking around the bed. She could hear the sound of his heavy steps in those boots. And then she felt his breath, warm on the side of her neck, his lips at her ear.

"*Punish the Slut*," he whispered. "It's my favorite game to play."

And then he lifted the cane and struck the first blow.

Light exploded behind her shut lids. She clenched down so hard, she thought she'd come right then. A second blow landed before she had a chance to absorb the first. Cold sweat ran down her spine. She bit so hard into the gag that the taste of rubber flooded through her. There was no way to scream, and yet the sound of her pain echoed in her head. A third blow crossed the first two, and she tested the bounds unintentionally, her whole body tensing, the handcuff chain rattling.

Four and five came in quick succession; a pause, then six, seven, and eight. She would have smiled if the gag hadn't been stretching her lips. He'd given her eight strokes for the time they'd planned on meeting. She heard the cane hit the floor and then she felt him on her, pounding into her, without a word, no kiss, just his cock inside of her, obliterating the pain with pleasure—almost, not quite, of course, but enough. There had to be a remnant of the pain—that's how Jamie was wired.

Killian had understood that about her from the start.

Some people just know.

He slammed against her, fucking her so hard she thought

she could feel his cock all the way to the back of her throat. She came when he did, spurred on by his climax, and then she felt the weight of him lift. But it was more than that. The weight of wanting lifted, the weight of needing, which had dogged her for weeks, urging her on, putting dark thoughts in her mind.

She was relaxed now—undone.

Tomorrow, she'd thank Roger for meeting her at the bar, buy him a dinner, maybe. He was a nice boy, a kid from the mailroom at work. She knew Roger and his boyfriend Daniel were hard up for cash, living from paycheck to paycheck. And maybe, if he asked really nice, she'd show him her marks in the ladies' room.

Punish the Slut.

Of course, she'd known the name of the game all along. But she hadn't wanted to win.

Not when losing was so much more her style.

MASOCHIST ON VACATION

Aimee Pearl

First things first. The night ended the way it did because Sir was practically begging for it, thrusting his hips into the bed and begging me to fuck him in the ass. Out loud, he hinted his desire in a somewhat benign way, as I massaged him. "You can massage my butt, too, ya know. There are a lot of muscles in there."

Sir and I are in complete agreement on this: I'm not a Top. But, on the rare occasions when I find myself in bed with another bottom, or a switch, or a Top who really can top from below, I know enough to know how to fuck someone in the ass. In fact, it's one of my favorite things to do.

So I took his hint and began kneading his ass. Although I had groped it once before, when he had jeans on, this was the first time in the six years since I met him that I was touching it bare. He had deliciously soft skin, and as I edged closer and closer to the middle, we both got more aroused.

But now let's back up. How did I get here? How did I find myself in Sir's bed, leaning over him, fingers teasingly making their way to that ultimate reward, that tight reservoir of joy? How did I get, in Sir's words, "so fucking lucky?"

It wasn't easy. This happened at the end of a long day of arduous physical labor and an unexpected amount of emotional labor, too. I was beyond tired—I was worn out. But I'd figured out a long time ago the value of taking pleasure in pain. And I'd delighted for years in Sir's particularly taxing forms of affection. Although definitions vary, I'm probably a masochist in some sense of word. And I was on vacation.

How It Came to This
It all started the previous month, when Sir came from the East Coast and stayed with me in San Francisco. In preparing for his visit, I asked him over email what kinds of foods he would like to have while at my house. I was earnest in my desire to be the consummate host, and I was ready to provide him with any amount of esoterica in the interest of catering to his whims. Flattered, he replied, "Are you sure you can't move to my city to be my housegirl?"

The thought intrigued me. Not the part about moving to his city; that wasn't going to happen, but being in his service, doing things for him, having no control or say in my movements, letting go. It would be like a vacation.

Sir was someone I felt I could trust. Submission is a delicate dance, especially when it comes to race. Although I'm not into race play, race inevitably enters the playspace—because we *have* race. I become especially conscious of racial differences when I'm with play partners who are white. The degree of trust that has to be present in submitting to a white person is significant. Sir had never let me down. I knew that his race politics were good, and I felt comfortable with the concept of doing domestic labor for him.

I feel the same about the idea of playing with Sir as a boy. In the email, he called me "housegirl," but my gender is maybe a little more fluid than "girl." At the same time, playing erotically with masculinity (even my own feminized version of it) is something that, being black, I have mostly only done with other people of color, specifically transgender men of color, with whom I feel safe exploring and expressing black masculinity. To be black and play as a boy is intensely charged for me. Sir, with his own nuanced relationship to his gender, both assigned and claimed, is one of the few white people I would play with in that type of headspace, because I have the feeling he *gets* it.

So I thought about Sir's offhand invitation, and considering the above, it really appealed to me. I had already made plans to come to Sir's city on a business trip the following month, and I would be staying at Sir's house during that time, a Thursday through Sunday visit. With that in mind, I asked Sir if he would like me to be in his service for the weekend portion of my trip (my business would be over by Friday afternoon). Happily, he said yes.

Preparation
In the weeks leading up to the assignment, I did a number of things to get ready. I consulted a friend who is in a 24/7 service relationship to his Daddy and got his advice on special touches I could do to go above and beyond, to please Sir. My friend suggested I research information on the supermarkets and drugstores closest to Sir's house, in case Sir needed me to run out and get something. He also said that mistakes would be inevitable, so I should take them in stride and be prepared to apologize and move on.

And my friend told me that, when he was first preparing to serve his Daddy, his preparation wasn't so much about learning to do specific tasks, as it was about spending time meditating on his devotion to his Daddy. I didn't know if I wanted to do something like that with Sir, because it sounded too crush-inducing. With Sir and I both having primary partners, getting a crush on Sir seemed less a good idea than a good way to get my feelings hurt. So I tried to let that suggestion go.

Next, I attended a workshop on service, at a leather conference. The speaker told me the best thing I could do to get ready for service was to bring Sir a gift that reflected his likes. Later that day, I spotted a brass paddle in the conference's silent auction. Gleaming and heavy, it called to me, and the moment I saw it, I thought of Sir. I didn't have much money, but luckily it had an extremely low opening bid, and only one other person had bid on it. So I beat that person's price by a dollar, and won.

After that, I did an online search for cooking tips. Sir has special dietary needs, and I wanted to make him some treats, cookies or cake, that would be edible for him. I read up on his diet, and I found a few recipes that would work, but they required hard-to-find ingredients. I called around to his local grocery stores but didn't find any within walking distance of his house that had the specific ingredients I needed. In the end, I bought those items in my own city and brought them with me in my luggage.

And while I was doing all this, I embarked on altering my body clock, to get on Sir's East Coast schedule. My goal was to be awake one hour before him, so that I would be ready whenever he needed me. I knew he was an early riser, while I'm a late one, so this was a particularly difficult task. I wanted to be able to wake up with ease at two a.m. my time, five a.m. his. My friend the service submissive warned me against this; he felt that it would be too exhausting for me, and that instead my aim should be to make the best of it that weekend, rather than tire myself out in the time leading to it. But I decided not to follow this advice, which, in the end, was probably a little bit of a mistake.

I got to the point where I could wake up easily by three a.m./six a.m. Beyond that, things were very hard. In the midst of this, I got a message from Sir saying that he would need me to be ready by seven a.m. his time on Saturday. That sounded doable. If I was up by six, I would have an hour to get ready for him. I continued to reach for two a.m./five a.m., though, so that I could get myself ready and have time left to bake him some cookies and brew his coffee—things he wasn't expecting.

Little Helper
I got to Sir's house with a cold. Between the body clock alteration and an illness that was going around my city, the traveling put me over the edge of being sick. On top of that, Sir has a cat and I'm allergic. It was hard to tell where the cold ended and the allergy began, because the symptoms were the same. It also didn't matter, because I felt like a stuffed-up, tired mess.

I was determined not to let that stop me from giving Sir a great weekend. Through stubborn will, I pulled myself together enough to be up by six on Saturday morning. I skipped the shower (I had showered the night before) and went straight to baking and brewing.

Sir had told me to be ready at seven, but he didn't come downstairs till eight. That was just as well, since the cookies took a little longer to make than I anticipated. While I waited in the kitchen, I ate breakfast and cleaned the dishes.

He showed up, and I instantly felt shy in that way I sometimes do around him. He's thin but looms large. He's resolute. I imagined he was born without self-doubt, or else just did something right in working on himself. I decided I could learn a lot from Sir.

Declining the coffee I'd made, he handed me an extensive list of chores and declared that today I would be called Little Helper. I had been secretly concerned about the issue of names, since neither houseboy nor housegirl really worked for me, gender-wise, and houseperson seemed too cumbersome. While I'm femme all the time, depending on the situation, I may be a femme boy or a femme girl. I was glad for a gender-neutral term like Little Helper, although it did instantly put in my mind that episode of "The Simpsons" where Homer brings home a pet dog named Santa's Little Helper. (Coincidentally, I had been thinking of telling Sir, if he asked, to call me Pet.)

I began to work. And in the mundanity of the chores—laundry, cooking, sweeping, vacuuming, mopping, et cetera—I found a rhythm, a place for meditation. I let my mind wander, over songs, TV shows, Sir's cock. Mostly his cock. And while I was thinking of his cock, twelve hours passed by, at the end of which, the house was spotless, more or less, and I was exhausted, much more than less.

Evaluation

At predetermined moments within that twelve hours, we met for check-ins, where Sir would ask me to evaluate my work thus far on a scale from one to ten, with ten being the top. I didn't feel that I could give myself a top score, because I had faltered on a couple of minor fronts. I had been late in making his breakfast, and I'd looked him directly in the eye once or twice. But I didn't want to give myself too low a score, at the risk of letting Sir think I wasn't proud of my accomplishments. And yet I didn't want to brag, in case I thought more of my work than he did. He's a mystery sometimes; I couldn't read him, couldn't guess at all what he was thinking of what I had done.

For our first meeting, I gave myself a six. By the next, a six point five. But at the third and final meeting of the day, I was distraught because I had forgotten one of his verbal instructions from earlier in the day, which was to give him a massage in between my vacuuming and mopping chores. The reason I forgot was because, while telling me massage instructions, he said that I was not allowed to give him a happy ending during the massage. I couldn't touch his cock no matter how badly I wanted to. Hearing him talk about his own cock was so distracting to me that I was unable to retain anything else from that conversation. So, after I finished vacuuming, I moved right into mopping, thinking about his cock the whole time, and not at all about the massage or its timing. Oops!

During our last check-in, however, he seemed less upset about the mishap than I was. He said that I had permission to make it up to him somehow. I had planned to give him the brass paddle the next day, at the end of service, which was scheduled to conclude after I made his breakfast. But considering the demands of the situation, I felt that now was the best time to give him the gift. Maybe he would use it on me to punish me for my mistake, and, in that case, we would both win.

He had mentioned that someone in service to him in the past had made mistakes on purpose, in order to provoke him into doling out punishment. That was shocking to me. *Why would anyone want to displease Sir?* My mistakes were innocent ones, and, during the day, I had beaten myself up over them. Hearing about Sir's other service experience was a big relief to me. It gave me permission to be imperfect.

He seemed very pleased with the paddle, which made my day. He had cooked me dinner. He instructed me to eat, bathe, and then come to his room. When I got there, the paddle was sitting on his dresser. I longed to feel it on my bare ass. Sadly, we never got around to that. But the pleasure was complete in the giving of the gift, so a paddling would have just been icing on the cake and was something I could live without.

Sir's Ass

In Sir's room, the massage he had waited all day for quickly gave way to me inside his ass. It was my first time fucking him. And maybe unfortunately for Sir—but definitely not for me— I'm something of a greedy fucker. Once I get in, I just want to go as fast as possible for as long as possible. I want to take someone fully and deeply. My fingers become my cock, and my cock is hungry. It's an unstoppable force. I'm not slow, I don't tease, I don't build up to a climax. I'm not a fingersmith. I don't have that skillful grace, that finesse and restraint, that intentionality to take someone on a crafted journey to orgasm. All I have is my desire, and my desire says, go deep, go deep, go deep.

I also never want to stop when a lover comes. Come once with me, and I'll want you to come again. I'll beg you to keep taking it for me, from me. And if I'm in your ass, I could stay there all night. I'll want to push in finger after finger, see how much you can take, see how many times you can come, see how long you can last. And I'll still outlast you. I'll want to exhaust you. I'll want to wear your ass out. I'll want to wear my arm out. I'll want to get you to the point where you say, "What am I, a hole?" and I'll say, "Yes, you motherfucking are."

After he came, I started petting him, compulsively, even after he asked me to stop. I was petting him like I wished, I realized, he had pet me, stroked me. I wanted to be his Pet, not just be called Pet. I wanted to be petted.

When we play, he's mean, and I appreciate that about him. But today hadn't been about play. It was work. I had worked for him. I needed niceness in these moments. I needed to be appreciated. He had given me praise for the work I'd done, and I clung

to each word he'd uttered. He'd told me that I did an excellent
job; that my only mistake was in the timing of the massage; that
the cookies were a treat; that the egg I made him for breakfast
was hard-boiled to perfection. I swam in the glory of his words.
I wanted to hear them over and over again.

I wanted to ask for what I wanted, but still shy, I held back. I
made a mental note to be more communicative next time.

Breath

I stopped petting him, we rolled over, and he sprang onto me. He
covered my mouth with one hand and pinched my nose closed
with the thumb and forefinger of his other hand. I was unable to
breathe. Startled and scared and wild eyed, I struggled against
him.

"Take it," he whispered, and in a flash, I was calm. I relaxed
into a state of knowing he would release me, he would let me
breathe again. He would control me, he would even own me in
a way. He would dictate the terms and conditions of my very
life, but just for that brief moment, just for that pause between
breaths, that moment when I couldn't breathe, that moment
when he held my breath in his capable hands. I trusted those
hands, and I trusted him.

He held my life in his hands when he took my breath away.
And knowing he would give it back to me, and that this was an
opportunity for me to show him just how much I trusted him,
made me sink even deeper into my own submission to him. As
he ran his fingers around the edges of my limits, I knew he could
even kill me. I could have died in his bed. This was the very edge
of edge play.

And so I was even just a little disappointed when he let go
a moment later. I could breathe again. It was over so quickly I
didn't even have time to feel like I'd run out of air.

And I say all this not because I have a death wish—not at all—but because I have a submissive wish. I wish to be his: naked, used, worked hard, and possessed, his.

Fist
Then he fisted me, getting me off twice. Sir inside me is an indescribable deliciousness. To feel his wrist stretching the entrance to my cunt, to experience the sting of being just-that-much too full, to be trapped by him even as I hold him in place inside me...that brings the orgasm that makes my whole body shake, that dances me across the bed, that moves me.

At some point in our tumbling fuck, my boxer briefs, which had been dangling precariously on the headboard, fell onto the floor between the bed and the wall. Delirious from my orgasms, I could barely walk, let alone pick them up. So when the shaking subsided, I put on my jeans and left Sir to fall asleep in his bed while I went downstairs to sleep on the couch, as I had been doing during my whole visit. It had been a long day for both of us.

Barter
By the end of the weekend, I felt closer to Sir. I felt that we were more intimate than before, because he had made himself vulnerable to me in a way. Not (just) in letting me fuck his ass, but in letting me do things like wash his clothes. Touching and cleaning his dirty laundry gave me pleasure that went beyond a kinky thrill.

I asked Sir if he would like me to serve him again sometime, and he said yes. He explained that it helps him to think of the service as a barter. I wondered what he felt he was bartering. Was it the sex? Was I cleaning his house in exchange for sex? That didn't sit right with me. I wanted him to want me, to desire me beyond just fucking me as a reward for mopping his kitchen floor. I wanted him to lust for me, to think of me and get hard, to see me in all my delicate strength and ache to be inside me, and maybe on occasion to have me inside him.

Was it the sadism? I wanted him to hurt me because he wanted to hurt me, because he got off on causing me pain, whether or not I had "earned" it with my labor. I wanted him to hear my breath catch, to see me wince, to listen to me beg him to stop, because it pleased him and got him off, and not for any other reason.

But his process is not something I have a say in, so I reconciled myself to being okay with him thinking it was a barter. I would continue to think it wasn't.

I realized that my lessons for next time were to remember: this is the place where I pamper myself, this is the place where I'm on vacation. This is where I luxuriate and relax in the knowledge of service, the cocoon of service. This is where I know that, no matter what I do, I'm doing a good job because I'm helping Sir, I'm alleviating Sir of work, I'm freeing up Sir's time to concentrate on other things, or nothing at all. And Sir is giving me time to be alone with my thoughts, to meditate on the beauty of a perfectly folded pillowcase, the expanse of a clean countertop, the shine of a polished wood floor—and my devotion to creating those things for him.

And suddenly the barter made sense, if what Sir was giving me in exchange was the opportunity to do for him, to be present in his life even after my flight departed. In *The Breakfast Club*, Ally Sheedy asks Molly Ringwald, after receiving an impromptu makeover, "Why are you being so nice to me?" to which Molly replies, "Because you're letting me," and both smile. Because he was letting me. That was our barter.

Epilogue

I've always felt great chemistry with Sir, even in moments where my shyness around him overtakes me and silences me. I feel like I can be a filthy pervert with him, and I get off intensely on making myself vulnerable to him. Even in writing this, I imagine showing it to him someday, giving him access to my thoughts and feelings, letting him see what he's inspired in me. Often with Sir, I feel at once too much and not enough. The intensity of my desire to submit to him embarrasses me, because I don't know if he feels the same amount of correlating desire to dominate me. And I don't know how to ask him, or how to change the way I feel, or how to express my feelings out loud. But I do know that he's allowed to see these flaws and dreams and insecurities in me; he's allowed to touch my rawness and read my words. In fact, I want him to.

I left Sir's house and headed to the airport. Having now officially lost my service cherry, I had a much clearer idea of what I wanted to do during service and in exchange for service. In retrospect, I realize that despite my teeth-gnashing over some very minor errors, I actually did an amazing job for Sir (especially, apparently, in comparison to his last houseboy). I came prepared, I went the extra mile, and I only made a couple of mistakes. But my cold and the day's work did wear me out, which compromised our playtime—I was so tired when we fucked. So I decided that next time, I would really make sure I was extremely well rested beforehand.

And as I landed in San Francisco, it suddenly dawned on me: my boy-panties remained unretrieved from behind his bed.

LIL' PET BRAT, AKA LILY GUANGLI

Kissa Starling

S ome think bratting is out-and-out defiance. Others say bratting is the term to describe a woman who misbehaves in order to get a spanking. If you ask me, it's just plain fun all the
way around. Being a good little girl can only last so long. Something deep inside demanded that I act out today and who was
I to refuse?

I strolled through the city mall with no particular purchase
in mind. Daddy insisted I get out of the house for a while. He always sensed when my mind had wandered and boredom had set
in. Window-shopping seemed to be my best bet for a hot Sunday afternoon. My thigh-high boots, loose shirt and short jean
skirt got me more than a few backward glances. If they'd looked
closely enough, they would have noticed the absence of my bra
and panties. Daddy never let me leave the house with them.

I wandered into the novelty store that had so many humor-
ous things. Shiny items enthrall me. A young, innocent version
of the future Daddy persuasion trudged around straightening

shelves. How cute. My own Daddy looked similar in his youth, before the lifestyle bug bit him in the ass. I ogled the clerk for a few minutes and then made a beeline to enter his vision. One had to wonder what occurrences in his life would or would not turn him toward becoming a Daddy in his own right. If I weren't otherwise taken, I might accept the challenge of training him myself.

"Can I help you with something, ma'am?" The twentysomething boy let his eyes travel up and down my chest, stopping on the birthmark that lay directly between my tits. I relished his attentions.

"Do you sell those fake piercing rings?" I batted my eyelashes at him while holding my fingernail on my lip, then drew it down to rest on my birthmark.

"Uh, yes, we have those. I recommend the sterling silver rings. They seem to last longer, and they don't leave marks on your skin."

You're teasing again, aren't you, pet? Don't tempt the little boy.

The voice reverberated in my ear. A reminder that Daddy never let me stray too far from his side. I looked all around but didn't see my Daddy outside the store. My bad, bratty choices had brought this on. The earpiece tickled my ear.

I slipped my shirt strap off of my right shoulder. My shirt fell forward so far that my nipple poked above the fabric, with my nipple ring outlining the front of my T-shirt.

"Where did you want to put the ring?" the clerk asked after wiping sweat from his brow. He changed his position and pulled the waist of his pants up, shifting his package.

Leave him now, Lily. You're here to relax, not flirt. Need I remind you—you're mine?

A horny young thing right here in front of me, and I had to

walk away. Thinking fast, I dropped my purse. Daddy should
have known I would get into trouble in public—I always did. I
sensed a setup.

"Let me help you with that." The boy dove down to retrieve
my purse. I leaned toward him. When he glanced up my bare tits
glowed right in front of his face. I shook them back and forth
and laughed because a vision of the last time Daddy played mo-
torboat entered my mind. It must have caught him off guard
because that's when he fell flat out on the store floor. His unin-
telligible muttering couldn't be deciphered. My jugs had power
over men and I loved it.

"Thank you for all your help. I'll come back some other day.
As you can see I have two real piercings already. Guess my clit
will have to wait." I reached down for my belongings, winked in
his direction and exited the store. The young clerk with a raging
hard-on gaped after me.

*You've pushed your limits once again, pet. For that you will
pay.*

I smiled to myself. Good thing they haven't invented a mi-
crophone that could read my mind. Otherwise Daddy would
know all of the times I tested *his* limits. How else am I supposed
to know just how far I can go before his domestic discipline is
administered?

Meet me in the food court.

"Yes, Daddy. On my way."

I hustled my tail to the next level, flirting with everyone I
passed. Daddy waited by the pizza place. Oh, goodie. He knew
how much I loved the Italian pie.

"Well, Lily. So nice to see you. I've already ordered for myself. Now you order." He handed me a ten-dollar bill.

I looked up at the menu deliberating my many choices. Veg-
gie with feta cheese looked appetizing.

"You're looking at the wrong menu, dear."

At first I actually looked around the food court, wondering if there could be another menu up for the pizza place. I gave him my best puzzled look and remained silent for further instructions.

"You will be eating at the hot dog vendor over there." He pointed across the mall.

My lip poked out and my eyebrows rose.

"Unless, of course, you don't want to eat."

I kicked the floor then took two of the ten steps that would lead me to the kiosk. After four more steps I turned to plead with my eyes. Daddy chose to speak in my ear so that no one else could hear.

"Now, Lily." I wanted pizza and hot dogs disgusted me. Of course, he knew that.

The hot dog vendor looked up at my approach. "What would you like today?"

"Apparently I need a long weenie to suck and chew and maybe vomit up later."

Lily...

"With mustard, please."

I almost felt sorry for the old man. He coughed and sputtered and handed me a hot dog so fast that I could only deduce he wished to get rid of me.

Go to the car.

Fine, I thought, *I'll go to the car, but not because you're telling me to—because I want to.* I'd pushed Daddy too far again. Craving all of his attention seemed to get me into frequent trouble.

You'd better be naked when I get there.

Oh, yes, he was definitely upset. My mind filled with trepidation on the trek to the car. Once inside, I removed my

clothing and held a jacket over my upper torso to hide my nakedness from passersby. I'd have to take my medicine this time.
I watched the doors of the mall, anticipating his arrival and nib-
bling on the mixture of ass parts. He strode through the doors,
took one bite of a piece of pizza and then threw the rest in the
can by the sidewalk.

Damn! My body stiffened. Locking the car doors passed
through my list of options but I rejected it immediately. Daddy opened the door and slipped behind the wheel. Without
even looking at me, he started the car and pulled away from
the parking spot. I snuck several glances his way but he didn't
look back.

"I'm sorry, Daddy. I know you don't like me flirting with
other men."

No response.

"It didn't mean anything anyway. You're the one I love."

Still no response.

We reached our home about five minutes later. "Go inside
and assume the position."

"Yes, Sir." At this point I'd become willing to suck up. I even
tried to kiss him on the cheek but Daddy turned away.

I sat, naked, on a wooden chair in front of the fireplace with
my back to the door. The door opened and closed behind me. A
peek would cause certain recrimination so I waited anxiously,
quelling all thoughts of future brattiness.

The refrigerator opened and closed. A pop-top got pulled
back. Just the sound made me thirsty. I doubted that throwing
back a cool one would be a viable option for me at that point.
Great, now I had to sit here and salivate over a beer! And I
didn't even like the taste of the nasty stuff. Daddy walked across
the floor, sat in his recliner and turned the television set on the
History Channel.

I wanted to pout but forced the inclination down. He knew I detested boring documentaries. Two hours later the TV got switched off. By some miracle of God I'd stayed in the correct position. My legs swung back and forth because I couldn't quite reach the floor unless I stretched my toes down. The urge to turn around grew.

Daddy came to stand in front of me. "A little brat is fun. A lot of brat is only fun for me." There was that evil smile of his again. He unhooked his belt from his jeans.

"Tell me what's going on."

My eyes drifted up to his face. "I need a spanking." There. I'd said it.

"Why didn't you ask for one earlier? We've talked about this, Lily. If you feel the need for discipline, ask for it."

"Yes, Sir. I just couldn't bring myself to ask. I don't know why." Tears welled up under my eyelids. I willed them away because I wanted my Daddy to be proud of me.

"Not only is that dishonest and disrespectful, it is also flagrant disobedience and that is something I will not have in this house... You know where to stand."

I stood up and walked around to the back of the chair, holding the back rungs with my hands and leaning my head forward, bracing myself.

Smack!

My punishment usually began with rubbing and small hits. The intensity of the first smack confirmed my suspicion that I'd gone too far this time.

Smack!

I clenched my asscheeks and held my breath for a few seconds. Once the pain and I became one, I expelled my breath and let the ol' asscheeks relax. My ass rose up in the air, seeking the slap of the black leather implement.

Smack!

Thoughts of being bratty and the everyday worries of life faded away. Erotic images filled my mind: Me and Daddy with our flesh close and rubbing together. Lips pressing together. Soft bites that lead down my neck. Soon my mind reached sub-space—the land of nothing and everything at the same time. In a distant land, a Daddy stood over his pet spanking her for severe misdeeds. Stress oozed from my pores to pool on the floor around me. All of the day's tension poured out in a rush. Fleeting thoughts of lyrics and good times passed through my consciousness but nothing stayed long. This was my safe place where nothing could touch me physically or emotionally. If only I could live in this special place.

Soothing touches caressed my bottom. I hadn't realized my eyes were closed until I opened them, peering up almost sleepily into my Daddy's eyes. My limp body lay across my Daddy's lap. He stroked my back and cuddled me close to him for quite a while. I basked under his attention and snuggled closer.

"I love you, pet. I'm so glad that you're in my life." His loving sentiments lulled me. I loved this part of the scene. My Daddy and I, in love and so connected.

After a while I decided that the time had come to 'fess up and let him know I'd fully returned, so I kissed his lips. This had always been our predetermined signal that I'd returned to full clarity. He returned the kiss, quickly taking control and sucking on my bottom lip. I shifted my body to sit upright in his lap and wrapped my legs around his torso. The fresh pain of punishment heated my bottom. His hands rested on both sides of my head and separated us.

"I'd like for us to talk about what led up to this, pet." He waited to ascertain my attention had turned to him.

"If you have a problem, come to me. I won't judge you or

punish you or hold anything against you."

"I know, Daddy."

"If asking for what you need is embarrassing, hell, send me a letter or better yet an email—instant satisfaction. It will beep right to my Blackberry."

"I was wrong to get my brat on once again. Sometimes I think my few minutes of bratting are a form of control for me. A snippet of taking charge of our relationship. I know that honor belongs to you and you alone. I apologize, Daddy."

"You're right in one respect, little one. Your brat behaviors are a form of topping from the bottom. Your job is to focus on my needs, not your own. Your faux defiance amuses me at times, but you must learn my hard limits." He paused.

"I know that you need discipline to take away the pressures of life. That's my job. I watch for the signs, but I must insist that you come to me if I don't see them or if they possibly are being hidden from me." His eyebrows rose as he spoke.

"So you knew how I tested you." I cast my eyes down to think for a moment. "My sole desire is to serve you, and I promise to think before I act next time. I will work on learning to identify the triggers that make me act this way as well."

"That's all I ask, pet."

Another day, another punishment. Ideas of how to be bratty tomorrow stormed through my mind. It's what I need to do, and I think Daddy knows that.

PLEASURE KEEPER

Charlotte Stein

You wouldn't know it to look at him. He has that casual, bed-headed look of all brothers of best friends everywhere, the sort of man who slinks into the kitchen while you're having a conversation and rifles through the kitchen cupboards, looking for the cereal. The kind of man who's far too old to be living with his parents, and yet somehow still is.

Like something washed up on a beach, that's how I thought of him. Like something left behind by adulthood.

Sheree hates him. She thinks he's a giant goofy jackass who shouldn't be allowed out in public. She thinks he's slow and stupid and mimics his slow stupid voice often. But then, all sisters hate their brothers. So it's not as though she's a reliable witness.

I should have known. I should have known he wasn't really slow or stupid or half as careless as he seems. He makes a ton of money from whatever Internet thing he does, holed up in his dank cave of a bedroom with the blinds drawn, bashing away at his collection of keyboards.

You'd think it would smell sweaty and faintly like come in there, but it doesn't. I know it doesn't because that's how all this nonsense started: I crept into his bedroom when he was supposed to be out doing god knows what and examined all of his things. Sheree was downstairs on the couch, asleep amidst the rubble of college applications.

She'll never apply. We've both been not applying for three years now. So I guess...well, how are we any better than Aaron? We certainly hadn't seemed any better when I stumbled over a great rubble of books stuffed under his bed, the sort of books I have to force myself to read. And then there were all the strange flickering things dancing across his many computer screens that made me think he wasn't quite as stupid as I had been led to believe.

And then there was his voice, not slow at all, cutting through the musty dimness, drawling right through me; kind of curious, just a little kink of curiosity in his stretching curling voice.

"What are you doing in here, Kitty-Cat?"

I recall imagining him down on his knees, trying to coax a timid little thing out from underneath the couch. *What did you get yourself into now, little pussy? Come out from under there and let me play with you.*

Despite the fact that he had just recently been out, he looked like he always did, like he'd just rolled out of bed. Too-long hair mussed, eyes sleepy, just a T-shirt and some pants that looked suspiciously like pajama bottoms. He's very tall. He looked very tall, right then.

I can't remember saying anything in reply. I think he said, "You like looking at my things?"

I don't know if he intended it to sound like a double entendre. Either way, it greased the wheels. It put certain things in motion that had not previously entered my head. I thought a lot about his big chocolate eyes and his equally big hands. I let him show me the website he'd been working on by crouching around me like a great warm spider, me perched on a stool and him behind.

He smelled like the pale green soap that comes in little wooden boxes, the kind you can get from any supermarket, all tangy and sharp. Not cloying, just sort of drifting over me.

It was all very good. I don't think he was hitting on me, exactly, but hey…if things went that way? I doubt he had plans to complain. He didn't complain at all when I simply turned my head and kissed him long and hard. I think it was all the warmth and his mussed hair and the tang of him.

But he kissed me back, even so. He said: "Are you sure you want things to go this way, Kit?" And in his voice there had been an odd note of laughter, a little liquid tease that tasted like hot chocolate going down.

"Sure," I said.

I should have known that you only ask a question like that if you're about to push someone until she pops.

It's an odd kind of thing. At first I had no idea he was doing anything at all. He seemed gentlemanly and if that meant that my trips to his bedroom and our illicit-for-no-reason dates ended with me feeling on fire, well, that's just how it should be. That's what grown-up dating is—we're adults, and adults don't wrestle with each other in the front seats of cars, trying desperately to get underwear off.

They wait for things to politely progress. By the third date I wanted to politely progress his entire body all over, up and down.

It was on the third that something awful struck me. As I lunged at him in the front seat of his stupid little Beetle car, and he tried to fend me off with all his "Whoa, whoas," I realized *I* was the jock, trying to get him to put out for *me*. He was the one always saying slow down, hold on, wait a minute.

But unlike me in that role, he laughed as he said it. He asked me in his caramel voice why I always had to be in such a rush.

I thought that was really cool of him. But it's looking less cool the more he does it. It's looking more and more like...like maybe this is his thing. He's a clit tease. A tormentor. He's getting off on making me suffer in ways I never thought I'd suffer with him. He's older and sure of himself and should be making me do every fucking thing under the sun.

And he's also becoming more and more attractive with every passing moment that we don't screw. He has a cumulative effect. Everything has a cumulative effect. The fact that we're sneaking around because he's my best friend's brother, the fact that his parents are often downstairs while we make out on his bed, the fact that he's as big as a house and swallows me whole when he's over me.

I'm now on a hair trigger. I get wet when he slides my coat down my arms. When he puts one knee between my legs and urges me back onto his bed. When he says, "Shh."

I'm already trembling. My cheeks are so hot I feel like I could burn him with them. When his body glides over mine and two layers of material graze my nipples, I kick out without meaning to. The covers ruffle up beneath my heels.

"What's the matter, Kitty-Cat?" he asks, but he asks it while he nuzzles that sensitive place just below my ear. He asks it while he's busy licking me with little flicks of his tongue. I stand on the edge of some sort of arousal precipice, just waiting for him to grasp a handful of one of my tits, to get both of his legs between mine and rut up against me.

"Nothing," I say, as I clutch at his back like someone drowning, drowning in a drought.

It doesn't help that he never kisses me the way other boy-friends did. His lips part softly over mine, in slow torturous rhythms that I can't follow. His tongue is lewd and slippery, thrusting into my mouth like a cock, just when I think he's going to tease. And then the other way around and again from the beginning.

I'm sorry that I didn't wear any underwear. I'm now so wet that it's all over my inner thighs, and I can feel myself all slick and swollen without even putting a hand down there. I honestly don't think I should try turning myself on any more than he already has done, but I have to. It's a compulsion. If I could just shift down on the bed, a little, I could rub my cunt against his thigh.

But he has me pinned. Too bad the pinning means that my tight tense nipples keep rubbing roughly against his chest, and that his hand keeps pretending that it's going to move down, to my thigh—and then slithers away at the last second. I could weep. I could beg. I think he might even want me to beg.

Though that thought does not help me.

He's moaning into my mouth, now. The sort of moan people make when they bite into something really tasty. And he's practically rocking against me, while his big hand cups the back of my head and clamps my mouth to his. I'm sure I can feel something thick and heavy, rubbing against my hip.

It's too much. I have to say something. I break away from all the kissing and push him up, up, but that is probably a mistake because his expression is one of single-minded hunger, eyes focused only on my mouth and his own mouth hanging open as though it was mean of me to deprive it.

But he doesn't force it. He waits. He's always waiting. That's the problem.

"Do you want me to blow you?" I blurt out. It seems like

the right thing to say. No man can refuse a hot wet mouth on his cock.

Only he just raises one thick eyebrow, and tickles one curl of my hair with a free finger.

"You're always in such a rush, Kitty-Cat," he says. "One thing at a time."

But I don't know what that means. Someone explain it to me. All the other guys were fucking me by now, jerking over me like broken marionettes, panting that I should come, I should come, I should come right now.

But he just sits up to the side of my body and strokes me all over with his gaze.

"Let's see what else we can try first," he says, and I praise God in my head.

He does nothing more than stroke one big hand down the sides of my body: first down one side, then the other, long languid strokes like he's buttering me, always getting close to tickling but never quite crossing that line.

When he finally and suddenly closes one hand around the underside of my right breast—firm, but not squeezing—it's a shock enough to make me squeal.

"Your breasts are so gorgeous. Look how they fit my hand like that," he says, and then he cups the other one, just to be sure.

I'm already juddering on the bed before he even gets to where he's apparently going next: steady circling massages that get closer and closer to my spiky nipples. They're standing right up through the material of my shirt, almost making shadows through the thin white material. And they're so sensitive that the massage alone is enough to spark little tingles of sensation from them to my clit, all that material chafing against the swollen tips.

I try not to whimper or groan. He already knows how eager I am, so I don't want to give him anything more. But when he finally, gently, pinches one nipple between his pulling thumb and forefinger, I want to cry. I want to cry harder when he asks me if I'd like him to put his hand inside.

I don't think I say coherent things. Him unbuttoning my shirt is the most exciting thing that's ever happened to me. My clit pulses and swells; I'm pretty sure I'm making a wet patch on the back of my skirt. I think I almost come when he slides his hand beneath the material of the shirt he doesn't spread open.

It's worse when he strokes my bare nipple, just softly, so softly. And then worse again when he takes his hand away and I whimper, and through his knowing smile he licks the pad of his thumb before oiling the stiff tip with that wetness.

I can't help it. I do moan, then. I moan and buck on the bed, desperate to touch my clit but sure that if I do, this will end. Nothing's been said, but I'm sure of it: if I break the slow crawl of all of this, he'll stop it. It'll be back to marionette jerking and *You should come, you should come*, I'm certain.

When he stops there anyway and tells me, "Second base is enough," I could kill him. I could scream. But that's when I know that this is how he wants it. His mouth curls into a teasing smile. This is how it has to be.

I don't touch myself, not even when I get back home.

The next time I see him it's worse, because I already know what to expect. The foundations of this whole thing are set, and so even when he takes off all of my clothes, one slow piece at a time, I know he's going to keep the pleasure from me.

I guess I should think he's just like those other guys, that he's selfish, and I probably would if he was constantly coming in my

mouth and in my pussy and all over me. But he never even takes
his pants off, so what am I supposed to think?

Not to mention the fact that when I'm lying on his bed completely naked, all he says are things designed to make me feel
good. I'm gorgeous and sexy and he wants to run his hands all
over me. And then he does just that, and I squirm beneath the
slick slide of his oiled hands.

I don't know why this is the next stage up from second base.
But I don't think I'm going to complain. I lay my head on his pillow and smell his green soap smell, and let myself be hypnotized
by the stroke, stroke, stroke of his hands.

He doesn't massage me, exactly. He explores, thoroughly,
and just when I think I'm relaxed and boneless rather than
turned on, all my nerves fire and tingle over into something that
makes me tremble. I shake like I'm coming, and in truth it kind
of feels that way. It's like an orgasm, only not, and all the while
he says: "Shh, shh."

But that's okay, because my body is singing. I can hardly
take it. Though I think he knows the truth: I can, I can.

He tells me to get dressed again in his drawling caramel
voice, so casual, teeth biting into his bottom lip. And I do, feeling sticky and oily inside my clothes, feeling stickier yet because
he watches me do what is only normal if it's reversed. He's lying
on the bed, watching me doing a backward striptease.

I think I can feel his eyes, pressing against my clit. It flutters
and protests, swimming in cream and as slippery as the rest of
my body is.

"I'll see you tomorrow, Kit," he says, and gives me a tender
kiss good-bye.

I don't touch myself when I get home.

* * *

Is this third base night? Is it more? I've lost track amidst all the
times when he's seen me completely naked, when he's showered
with me and soaped my aching body, when he's licked pieces of
fruit from my belly button.

He sucked my nipples last night. Tremors ran through me,
like an orgasm, again, like, but not quite. He had his leg between my thighs, and I think I soaked through the thin material
of his pajama bottoms.

Not that he minded.

And now we're on his bed together, kissing hungrily. Swirls
of sensation form pits and pools in my belly, just by my thinking
of what he might have in store tonight. This might be it. This
might be the one.

In fact, I'm sure it's going to be, until he actually does something. Then I'm simply stunned that he's finally crossed that
line. He has his hand up my skirt. His hand is high up, on my
inner thigh.

I'm still not prepared when he tells me to take my skirt off.
Though as with everything he does, it isn't exactly an order. It's
laid back, calm, soft.

And as ever, I rush to do what he hasn't ordered me to do.

I kick the thing down my legs, briefly embarrassed that I'm
not wearing any underwear, that I now never wear underwear
when I'm around him, but too far gone to care. I was too far
gone weeks ago, why should I care about anything now?

He covers my entire mound with one huge hand. I moan like
I've never moaned for anyone before. I moan and urge myself
up, up against him. I'm so wet that one push in the right direction will part my pussy lips easily.

But he's wise to that game. He lets his hand hover, sometimes finely brushing the damp curls there before moving away.

He gives me the illusion of having those swollen lips touched; he traces and stirs the air around me and waits for me to moan again.

When I do, he murmurs something I wish I could record. I don't even know why.

"Oh, so *responsive*," he says, and I sob into my hands.

He uses just the tip of one finger to seek out my secret slit, to run along that seam without ever really plunging in. For the first time, I am desperate enough to come close to grabbing his hand. I need to force him on me. I need to beg him.

But I take deep breaths through the spaces between my fingers and get myself under control.

My reward is a deeper sort of stroke, his thick thumb spreading my folds open. He avoids my aching, tingling clit, but the stroke over all my heavily sensitized flesh sends pleasure messages directly to it. My cunt clenches and clenches around nothing.

"Do you usually get so wet, Kitty-Cat?" he asks me, but he must know that I can't speak. He's looking directly at the heart of my sex, leaning down so that he can see me spread and soaking for him. I feel his hot breath ghost over my stiff bud and I gasp out his name.

"Do you get this wet when you masturbate? Does your clit get so swollen? I bet you can hardly stand me to touch it..."

Of course, when he does, I jerk for him. I jerk, like a marionette.

But I don't come. Not quite. I'm so close that I can feel the wavering edges of it, low down in my belly. I can feel its collar around my neck, getting ready to tug. And when he moves away from my clit and eases through all of my slippery honey to my still-clenching hole, I almost choke on my own frustration.

I don't come even when he slides two fingers right into me

to the hilt, and the sound I was going to make turns into a long drawn-out groan.

"Do you like that?" he asks, and I'm sure his head is cocked to one side. It's equally possible that he has an eyebrow raised. However, I can't take my hands from my face to get a proper look.

If I lift them from my eyes, if I move even an inch, he might stop. He might not give it to me.

"It seems like you like that. I can feel you tightening around me. And you're so wet, so wet and swollen, especially...especially right...here."

He twists his fingers inside me, curling them just so before rubbing and rubbing like I've got an itch. There's this itch right down deep in my sex, and he's going to soothe it nice and slow.

Only I can't go nice and slow. It's far too late for that. Slow is everything that's come before this and now he's fucking my cunt with two thick fingers, urging them right against my G-spot like it's just. That. Easy.

And oh, Jesus H. Christ, when he bends his head and his hot breath pours deep and rich right over my clit, I could—I'm definitely—oh, yes, it's there. Oh, go on, ah, yes. And then ah, no, when his wicked pointed tongue flicks out and just barely flicks over the bursting tip of my aching clit.

It's barely anything, really—enough, though, to make me come all over his hand.

And I do, god, I do. I come in great wrenching spasms, my cunt creaming while my body goes rigid, the sounds out of my mouth like something animals refuse to do. I grunt and twist and try to get away from it, it's so dense and all consuming. Something rips in my fist and I'm dimly aware that I've just ruined his bedsheets, but he only laughs as he works me on his fingers, rough and slow.

He's made me too hungry now, though, far too hungry, and I go up for another before the first is even finished. I'm still moaning and twisting on the bed when he replaces his fingers with his cock, jeans rudely shoved to his knees, the sudden thickness a slap to my senses that I can hardly take.

I buck against him crazily, but he's too heavy and suddenly, gloriously insistent for it to throw him off his stride. He fucks into me hard, urgently, one hand grasping at the headboard to give him that extra bit of leverage.

I'm still so swollen and thick with pleasure that it seems as though I can feel every inch of his cock, the cock I've never actually seen. I try to flutter my pussy around its gorgeous length, but there's no room to spare.

He gasps for my troubles. He wavers out words, too. "Jeez, this isn't going to last long."

That, I can't do anything but laugh over. I feel it bubbling up inside me, mad hysterics that need out. What does he mean? This has lasted forever and ever and ever; isn't it a hundred years since we started?

When he reaches down between our bodies to touch my clit, I almost slap his hand away. No more, please, no more. Even if I want more—please, no more.

He doesn't listen. I guess he doesn't have to, when he never needs me to say a word. He circles my clit messily as his cock pumps in and in and in, and when I finally stretch one last fantastic time, when I pant and fuck up against him and call out his name too loudly, he does the same right back at me.

I feel him swell inside me. He groans out: *So good, so good, right there.*

And then it's over. It's over.

* * *

I want to ask him what his game was, as we lie side by side in his narrow bed, comfortably silent and cooling down in the autumn air that's leaking in from the window. But I don't think he'd give me a good explanation.

It's like he kept all of my pleasure in a little jeweled box, and when I was ready, when I was beyond ready and into delirious, only then did he show me what was inside. That's what I keep on thinking, as he brushes careless fingers over the inside of my arm.

I suppose I should be disappointed, now. All those treasures, all used up. All that buildup, laid to waste, pulverized by an orgasm so intense, I can still feel it running through me.

Thankfully, he has a solution. I should have known he would. He's too sly and teasing not to. Just as I'm drifting off to sleep, he turns his head on the pillow, eyes lit with evil intent.

"Think you might want to try it the other way around?" he says, and I flash on the other boys, the other boys always trying to get what they want and never giving me what I need. But he's not like that, Aaron isn't. It's a different sort of game altogether, with him. He can hide his desires so easily that I've got no idea how long I could draw it out with him, or how far I'd have to go.

"Yeah," I tell him. "Yeah, I can do that."

WELCOME TO
THE WORLD

Ariel Graham

She woke in the cage, which disoriented her. The last time she'd slept in it had been over a year ago.

Once, the cage had been a bolt hole. Somewhere Lisa went when the world closed in on her and she needed to feel she could give up everything and let someone else take care of her.

But gradually it had changed, become only erotic, only against her will or at least against her will in appearances and maybe not at the times of her choosing.

And then they'd backed off. Mark got a job that required commuting and Lisa got a job she loved and the cage became a kind of strange, oversized bedside table.

She'd spent last night in it, though.

Warm morning sunlight fell over her through the bars. Her body felt sore and languid, well used.

She craned her neck. The alarm had gone off—that's what woke her—and Mark's side of the bed was empty.

Why am I in here on a workday? she thought.

Which was when she remembered: talking late into the night, agreements reached, past disappointments broached and forgiven, a new start intended.

Yes, but.

She looked at her watch, which she still wore, a digital with a cheap band, stark against her otherwise naked flesh.

Late. She was going to be late. "Mark?"

He stuck his head around the bathroom wall. "Good morning, sunshine." He foamed at the mouth with toothpaste and good cheer. Mark looked like a little boy half the time, all tousled brown hair and innocent eyes. She was always amazed he could turn into her Master in a heartbeat.

But he hadn't, for so long.

She swallowed, drily, and her voice was weak when she said, "I'm going to be late—?" and it became a question. They'd talked about her work. She loved her work. She worked at a bakery and floral shop, made beautiful cakes and flower-shaped cookies and sometimes candy and did some flower arranging, and her boss wasn't great but wasn't terrible. What had they decided? Mark, who worked from home, had said something about bringing her back home, having her less out of the house: less visible, more his.

But she hadn't agreed, had she?

"Did we drink last night?" She was so fuzzy.

Mark grinned down at her in the cage, sitting naked on the bed just out of reach. His cock sat up all by itself, all morning-happy and moist from the shower. Beads of water glistened in the darker hair on his balls. She wanted to bury her face there, quench the weird nervous thirst with his shower water and suck him into her throat.

"Mark?"

"I called you in sick today. Can't have a sick chef."

"Baker."

"Sick chef. Say that six times fast."

"Mark—"

"No," he said. "Say it six times fast."

Lisa shut her mouth. They'd slid into Game and she'd missed the signal.

Unless there wasn't one.

No signal? Was that what they'd discussed?

"Lisa."

She said it, six times fast, and yes, at the end it sounded more like "shish shush" and that was fine, she'd always sucked at tongue twisters. She had other things on her mind now.

"Good girl," he said, and sat down again. "So. No. We weren't drinking last night. We had too much to talk about for that. Do you remember?"

No. She remembered a long talk, about what they'd had, what they wanted, but... "We didn't just talk?"

He grinned then. "That's why you're so spacey. You were flying. Very high."

But she wasn't sore. She was, actually, but only in a few spots, which meant he'd taken very good care of her and all that soaring, flying, wonderfulness had been caused by being restrained.

Because when he caused it other ways, parts of her remembered promptly.

Lisa stretched as best she could in the cage. Despite the strange distortions of the morning her body felt languid and relaxed. Her mind snarled like a rat in a trap, looking for what menaced it and left her speeding, sensing danger.

"Mark? You didn't *quit* my job, did you?" She held her breath. Life was a balance. Anything could topple it. She knew what he wanted, and she thought she could stand being more isolated, more *his*, but the job wasn't social, the boss was a boss, the other baker a bitch, the customers only transactions.

"I put that on hold. You can keep the job as long as you abide."

Panic and relief raced through her and left her dizzy. She still had her job.

...abide by *what?*

He let her out midmorning when she begged to use the bathroom. He put her on the treadmill for thirty minutes at a pace she could sustain and worked until she finished her run, then sent her to shower and when she stepped out of the shower, he'd drawn a low tub of hot water he motioned her into. Lisa lay back apprehensively and Mark said, "Bring your knees up and spread your legs." He held up shaving cream and a safety razor.

"No, Mark, please, I hate that," she started and he knelt beside the tub and put a hand over her mouth.

"You really don't remember last night."

She could feel how wide her eyes were. She shook her head.

"We're going into World for a while. You agreed to try. You couldn't quite say the word *slave* but you agreed to be a complete sub, in and out of the house. Do you want to see the notes and the agreement we drew up, or—"

She shook her head. Memory flooded back, and along with it the fact that they'd had their discussion—most of it—and made their agreement—all of it—after he'd sent her flying.

He watched the changes she could feel crossing her features. When she met his eyes again, he said, "Spread your legs."

Lisa spread her legs. She watched in the mirror he'd set up on the edges of the tub as he lathered her pussy and shaved away the soft red-blonde hair, then went over it and over it, fingers and razor, feeling every hair, until at last he ordered her out of the tub onto her hands and knees and then over the edge of the tub. "Hold your asscheeks apart," he said, and he lathered her there and went to work until her ass and cunt were revealed, clean and naked and glistening.

She stood and he knelt on the bath mat in front of her and touched her, spreading her lips, using his thumb to push her clit up and back. "That's mine," he said, his voice husky rather than demanding. "All of that is mine. Turn around and bend over."

She whimpered but complied and he spread her wide, just looking. Breathing. Owning.

"Go lie on the bed. On your stomach. Hands behind your back."

And she remembered everything from the night before.

He knelt behind her on the bed and she felt him slip handcuffs around her wrists before she could protest. She hated handcuffs, preferred almost anything else, which was why he used them.

That, and they were secure.

"Lie still," he told her. "And no talking. No sounds."

She lay, head turned on the pillow, her hands cuffed on the small of her back, and wondered how it could still be humiliating to have him do this to her.

"Spread your legs," he said. His voice sounded husky.

Lisa moved them apart, widely, as would be required, and felt him shift on the bed. The sound of a jar opening reached her and then she felt something cold and slick against her asshole and she froze, then thrashed wildly. Somewhere deep in her mind an observer whispered she wasn't making a sound and how strange to comply in part but only in part.

"Lisa." His voice harsh, strident. This was her Master.

She bucked against him. *This* was the exact minute they'd stopped all those months ago, when she'd walked out of the

Game and back into reality without a safeword or a discussion or a compromise.

Because there were aspects she loved about the idea of being owned: Sex at odd hours. Calling him Sir. Spankings and discipline. She loved being restrained, for reasons she had no interest in understanding. Hold her down and fuck her from behind and she went wild. Cuff her hands behind her, throw her onto her back and screw her till they both came and she was multiorgasmic. Tie her to the bedpost and play with her, blindfold her—and she flew.

But it was Game. Because she could and did say No. No safeword, just No. She hated him examining her, looking close. She hated being shaved. She wasn't crazy about toys and all of that she could control.

She'd heard it called topping from below and she was good with that, damn it. Mark loved their sessions, spanking her, restraining her, her wildness, his control.

But it was a game. And when it went too far, she stopped it.

But this: they'd discussed this ever so long ago, and again, last night, when she was out of her mind with pleasure.

This wasn't Game. This was World. And she'd stopped it before.

She thrashed. She kicked and bucked and wriggled and tried to force her way out from under him.

Mark moved. His weight came down over her hips. She could feel how hard he was as he leaned forward and pressed her shoulders into the bed. He lay his body against hers, riding out her storm, keeping his weight off her cuffed hands by holding her shoulders down.

When she torqued again he forced her down and now he knelt, hands on her shoulders, one knee in the small of her back.

He whispered directly into her ear, two words.

"Lisa. Submit."

She went still and then limp. Reverse safeword. Game slide. They'd put it together when they first started. At any time, in any place he said, he could whisper it to her and she'd comply.

But he never had.

It had been a *game*.

She took a long shuddering breath and then another. Her body relaxed by degrees. She spread her legs again and lay still.

Mark moved off of her, gradually, waiting to see if she'd fight again.

But this was when she'd made him stop before.

Mark knelt between her legs again. Something cold and slick touched her asshole. Mark's hand came down, deftly separating her asscheeks. He pressed the cold gel against her and inside, and then more, and then more. Lisa bit back a groan and Mark paused, then slid his finger deep inside her and pressed into her, fucking her gently with one finger, slow. Lisa bit her lip and tried not to protest, squeezed her eyes shut—tried to go away.

"Stay with me," Mark ordered into her retreat, and the finger went away and was replaced. It was a long, slim, straight dildo—she could almost picture it, thought she'd seen it recently, out of the corner of her consciousness—and he slid it inside her, slow, so she'd feel it moving into her, inside her, an inexorable claiming of her most private place.

"I'm going to fuck you there," he whispered. "It's going to get bigger and bigger until you can take all of my cock in your ass. We're going to train you, the way we talked about last night. Do you remember?"

No, not clearly, she didn't. But it didn't matter. Something was building: a heat, deep inside her, an ache to be filled even while he kept the thing pressing deep inside her. And then he

pressed the whole of his palm over her clit and cunt and moved
it very fast while he slid the dildo deep into her ass.

"Come. Hard," he whispered.

And Lisa obeyed.

She went back to work two days later, on the condition she understood and would abide. And now she knew what there was
to understand and what she needed to abide by.

She was his. In the late hours of that one night, after flying
and coming partway down, she'd signed an agreement with him
to go into the World for a year and a day. She'd given herself to
him. Her concessions were enormous. She'd given up the right
to wear clothes at home unless given that permission and that
included should Mark find like-minded couples to hang out
with. She could wear underwear to work, where she thought
she was required by law to, but nowhere else. At home, he could
cancel any of her appointments or call her in sick as long as
she didn't lose her job. She would be naked, his to command,
often plugged, always well fucked, whether by him or not. He
could share her and claimed he would. He could photograph
her body without her face and post the photos online. And the
discipline—

Lisa marveled.

On the other side of the agreement were Mark's concessions,
both of them: *I will not harm you. I will not allow you to come
to harm.*

And that was that.

Her ass was his, to train, to fuck. Her body was his. Her discipline was up to him. Her sense of responsibility, the way she
was always wherever anyone expected her to be—was his.

She went to work two days later, in a bra lined with Velcro,
the scratchy receiving parts of Velcro. She wore a thong two

sizes too small snugged deep into her crack. And when she got home, he promised her a spanking that would stop her from sitting.

She'd promised to go to the house on her lunch break and to not talk much at work and Mark in return had promised not to make her quit her job. Yet.

"Are you okay, Lisa?" her boss asked when Lisa spilled the third vase of flowers for the day.

"Just clumsy," Lisa said, and could barely stop herself from grinning. Because everything was absolutely perfect in her world.

STROKE

Lisabet Sarai

N o."

I nearly jumped out of my sensible shoes at the unexpected command. I whirled to check the motionless figure stretched out on the bed behind me. "What?"

"Don't close the curtains. I want to watch the moon's progress." I glanced back at the window. Sure enough, the silvery orb was just climbing above the silhouettes of the trees surrounding Lindenwood.

"Very well, Mr...." I squinted at his chart in the dimness. "Carver." Jonathan Carver, age sixty-four, acute right hemispheric CVA. Hemiplegia, nystagmus, transient apraxia, reduced peripheral vision in left eye.

"It's Dr. Carver. Don't they brief you damned nurses? Teach you some respect?" Even as I bristled at his rudeness, my cheeks grew warm with inexplicable shame. His cultured voice held an authority that brought me back to my school days. Mr. DeFazio and his infamous blackboard pointer. Tears in the eyes of the students naughty enough to merit his punishment. I was always good, obedient and hard working, but I remembered the heat of watching.

"Sorry, Dr. Carver." The man fumbled with the bed control, trying to raise himself to a sitting position. "Let me help you."

"I can do it myself." A frown furrowed his high forehead, under a shock of steel gray hair. It took him three tries to get hold of the button, even with his right hand. Clearly there was some bilateral damage. His lips pressed together. His chiseled features twisted in concentration. At last, the motor whirred and the back of the bed rose six inches. He sank back into the pillows with a disgusted sigh, scrutinizing his recalcitrant fingers. He had big hands, hands that looked as though they'd once been strong.

I smoothed and straightened the coverlet, trying to hide my pity and embarrassment. "Are you more comfortable now?"

He brushed me away. "I'll tell you when I need help," he growled. "Hopefully, you can follow basic instructions."

"I'll do my best." Something about his manner made me blush and stumble. I felt an acute desire to please him, to show him that I was competent and eager to tend to his requirements. Clearly he was accustomed to giving orders.

I tucked the sheet in around his feet, untwisted the cord leading to the bed control and gathered the used paper cups from his bedside table. I needed to be doing something. His silence made me increasingly nervous.

"Enough, enough! Stop fussing and turn on the light. Let's see what you look like." His voice held all the power that his body had lost. I rushed to the switch, a flock of crazed sparrows fluttering in my stomach. "Come here, girl."

I stood by the chrome railing, staring at my scuffed nurse's shoes, sweat gathering in my armpits and under my breasts.

"Look at me." His tone was softer but no less firm. I raised my eyes to his, which were the startling blue of glacial ice. I shivered and burned. "You're new, aren't you?"

"Yes."

"Yes, Sir," he corrected me. My nipples tightened inside my bra.

"Yes, Sir." Just his voice was enough to make me ache.

"What's your name?"

"Cassie, Sir. Cassie Leonard."

"Don't look away, Cassie. Look at me. Do you know who I am?"

"No, Sir. I just started at Lindenwood this week. Before that I was in the rehab department at Miriam Hospital."

"My slaves call me Master Jonathan."

My earlobes, my nipples, my fingertips, all seemed to catch fire. I wanted to sink through the floor. I didn't want him to see how his words excited me.

But he did see. I stared at my hands, knuckles white from gripping the rail.

"You have a boyfriend, don't you?"

"Yes, Sir, I do." An image of Ryan rose in my mind, his brown curls and uneven grin, muscled chest and hard thighs. I did love him, truly I did, with his quirky humor, his gentle fingers and his boyish ardor. He was a fine young man. My mother approved of him.

"He doesn't satisfy you." It was a statement, not a question. Tears of remembered frustration pricked the corners of my eyes. "Why not, Cassie? Is his cock too small?"

I couldn't believe I was having this conversation with a stranger, a patient, a half-paralyzed man forty years older than I was. I stole a glance at Dr. Carver. His mouth was firm but his eyes sparkled with suppressed mirth.

"No, Sir. His cock is fine." Ryan was justifiably proud of his meaty hard-ons.

"What is it then? Is he a selfish lover? Does he come too quickly for you?"

Guilt washed over me. Ryan would happily spend hours licking my pussy and fingering me, trying to get me off. The only way I could manage it was to think about scenes from the kinky porn I hid from him, whippings and spankings, gags and handcuffs, all the clichés that I couldn't stop myself from wanting.

"Well? Tell me, Cassie. What do you need that he doesn't provide? What do you want?"

My mouth filled with cotton. I couldn't speak. I was acutely aware of my rigid nipples pressing against the starched fabric of my uniform. My clit pulsed like a sore tooth inside my sodden panties.

"Cassie, I'm waiting." His sternness sent electricity shimmering through my limbs. "Don't disappoint me."

I dared a glance at his face. His left eyelid drooped slightly. His eyes snared mine. I couldn't look away. One eyebrow arched in an unspoken question.

"I—um—I want him to, uh, to do things to me. That he doesn't want to do." I tried to break away from his gaze, but the force of his will held me.

"Things?" He sounded amused. A fresh wave of hot, wet shame swamped my body. "What sort of things?"

"Uh—tie me up. Spank me. Use me. Treat me like his slave." It all came out in a rush, the desires I'd never shared with anyone except Ryan. Even then, I'd only shown him the tip of the iceberg, the least perverted of my needs. "He wouldn't, though. He was shocked when I told him. Disgusted. Said that I had a filthy mind." The tears that had gathered earlier spilled out over my cheeks.

"I imagine that you do, little one, delightfully filthy." His voice was a caress, soothing and seductive. "I knew that right away, just from your reactions to my voice. Your deepest desire is to submit to a strong master, isn't it?"

"Yes—Sir." I felt relief, now that I'd admitted my secret. At least he didn't seem to condemn me.

"You want to be beaten and buggered, shackled to the bed and split open by a huge cock. You want to bathe in your master's come, maybe even his piss. To be forced to service his friends."

It was thrilling and horrible, listening to him enumerating my darkest fantasies out loud. My clit felt the size of a ripe plum, swollen and juicy, ready to burst. I nodded, still finding it difficult to expose myself so completely.

"I will do those things for you, if you'd like."

"You?" The suggestion startled me enough that I forgot the honorific, but he seemed to forgive my lapse. I searched his handsome, ravaged face. "How...?"

"Don't underestimate me, girl. I may not be the Dom I once was, but I can still make you burn for my touch. I can still make you beg." He snagged the button on the end of its cord and raised himself to full sitting position. He moved more smoothly and easily than before. "Remove your clothing."

I just stood there, petrified by mingled fear and excitement. If anyone discovered us, I'd lose my job. I'd never work as a nurse again. Five years of education down the drain. But this might be my only chance. The chance to make my fantasies real.

"Didn't you hear me? I told you to strip."

"Uh—yes, yes, Sir." I tore two buttons off my blouse, struggling to remove it. I tripped and nearly toppled onto the bed while wrestling with my trousers. When I unfastened my bra and released the weight of my breasts, Dr. Carver let out his breath in a long, appreciative sigh. A little thrill of triumph sang through me. He wanted me. My Master wanted me.

I slid my soaked bikini over my hips and down to my ankles. The sea-soaked scent of my pussy rose around us. I would have been embarrassed if I had not been so aroused.

"Give them to me." I put the damp slip of cloth in his open palm. He brought it to his nose and inhaled deeply. "Lovely. You're already wet, from simple anticipation. Wait until you experience real pain." He reached for one of my aching nipples and pinched it until I yelped.

"Go get a pair of forceps from that drawer under the sink." I scurried off and returned with the article he'd requested. I wondered how he knew where the medical instruments were stored. Could it be that he had seduced my predecessor the same way as he overwhelmed me? I didn't have time to be jealous, though. He caught my left nipple in the jaws of the forceps and clamped down hard.

Pain raced from my tortured breast to my pussy, transmuting to pleasure on the way. The harder he squeezed, the more tightly my cunt clenched. Fresh pussy-juice gushed from my cleft. I moaned, struggling to stand as he gradually increased the force of his grip.

"Do you like that, girl?" He released the inflamed left nipple and captured the right, sending new pangs arcing through me. I trembled, panting, unable to answer even if I dared. "You don't need to tell me. I know you do. You'll like it even more when I clamp your fat red clit." I came close to exploding at the obscene image. My cunt spasmed. My whole body shuddered. "I can't wait to hear your screams."

The pressure on my nipple disappeared. Echoes continued to ripple through me. "Turn around. Spread your legs. Let me see your ass."

My only desire was to please him. I turned and bent at the waist, gripping the back of a chair near the bed. "Beautiful," he murmured. "Your sweet white skin will mark nicely." His fingers trailed lightly across my backside. I arched back, thrusting my bottom toward the bed and silently begging for more.

"I think that the first time I beat you, I should use a riding crop. Each stroke will hurt more than the last. The pain of a crop is sharp, searing, biting deep. Eating into you, body and soul. I'll beat you into a lather, my little pony. Your ass will look like it has been barbecued. You won't be able to sit down for days."

I could see it all. I wanted it all, wanted it now. The delicate trace of his fingers on my flesh burned like the trails of fire he promised me. His silken voice made me weak with desire. My clit was a red-hot coal threatening to burst into flame.

"Touch yourself, girl. Show me how much you want to be my slave."

I didn't think twice. Before my new Master, I knew no shame. I brushed my palm over my sticky pubic curls, then slipped my middle finger into my soaking cleft and grazed my clit. Lightning shot through me. My body began to erupt. He rested his palm on the small of my back, short-circuiting the climax.

"Cassie! Don't come, slave. Not until I tell you that you may. Can you do that for me?" His voice was gruff with lust. Joy sang through me at the realization. He wasn't doing this just for my benefit.

"Yes, Sir." I managed through gritted teeth. I pulled back, sliding my fingers along my slippery lower lips, avoiding the swollen nub begging for my attention. Sensations prickled and sparked between my thighs. I spread myself wide with one hand and stroked with the other. The Master's magic fingers returned to my butt, kneading and caressing. I strained for control.

"Before your first flogging, I'll rope you up and suspend you from the ceiling. Wrists fastened together, arms pulled overhead. I'll secure a spreader bar between your ankles, to keep your thighs apart and make sure you're accessible. I've got a fine cat that I'll use to whip your shoulders, your back, your butt—strokes fast and then slow, each one slicing across your lovely pale skin and leaving fiery trails. When you can't take any more, I'll just twirl you around and start on your breasts and your belly. Every so often I'll stop to use one of your holes. Your mouth. Your dripping cunt. Your tight, tender ass. I'll fill you with my come. Then I'll go back to beating you."

My fingers squelched in my cunt. I thrust them deep, trying to get my whole hand inside. My clit throbbed and twitched. I felt the orgasm coiling deep in my pelvis, winding tighter and tighter as his words and his stroking hand drove me toward the edge.

"The marks will show the world that you're mine. I'll take you out to my favorite club, lead you collared and naked through the crowds, so that everyone can admire the rosy tattoos of your devotion. Don't stop frigging yourself, girl. Work those fingers. In and out and around. That's right."

I hovered near the peak of pleasure, dizzy, pulsing, terrified that I would topple over the precipice and disappoint him. I focused on his hand, still dancing across my butt, and his deep, controlled, hypnotic voice, painting pictures that seemed more real by the minute.

"Everyone will want a piece of you. I'll drag you up onstage and bind you to the padded horse. Then, one by one, the mistresses and the masters will take you, however they choose. Paddling you, whipping you, clamping your clit, forcing their fists into your cunt. You'll take them all, for me, and you'll love it, won't you, my slutty little girl. Won't you?"

His finger traced its way into the cleft between my buttcheeks.

I held my breath, unable to move, unable to answer.

"Finally, at the end of the night, when you've been beaten and fucked to exhaustion, I'll stand behind you, grab your hips, and ram my cock into your ass. And then I'll let you come. I'll pump myself into your butt and we'll come together, master and slave.

"Come now, Cassie. Come now!"

He pushed his slick finger deep into my rear hole. One finger only, I knew it was just one finger, but I felt the thickness of his cock, the pain of being stretched, the dirty joy of being filled, the spasms as he emptied his seed into my bowels. I was there with him, in that club he described so vividly, jerking and convulsing as I came, impaled on my Master's cock.

The tension snapped. Fierce gusts of pleasure battered my body. I sank to my knees, face against the padded seat of the chair. It went on and on, swells of sensation spiraling up from my sex, shaking me until I was limp and exhausted.

The quiet finally roused me. I stood up, stiff and sticky, and turned to face Dr. Carver. He lay back against the piled pillows, his eyes shut, locks of silvery hair plastered to his forehead with sweat. He was completely still. The sheet barely moved with the rise and fall of his shallow breathing.

Oh, my god! What had I done? What if he had suffered another stroke? I groped for his wrist. His pulse was slightly elevated. I cursed myself and my unnatural desires. I'd lose my license, certainly, but that wasn't what mattered. My only concern was for my Master.

"Master?" I whispered. I grabbed him by the shoulder. "Sir? Please, Sir, wake up. I'm so sorry, Sir..."

His sapphire eyes flipped open. He favored me with a faint smile. "Don't be sorry. I'm fine, Cassie." He placed his hand on mine, stroking a fingertip along my wrist and sending shivers up my spine. "Better than I've been for months." Warmth flooded

STROKE   161

through me as his voice gained strength. "Now, put your clothes back on. Then you can help clean me up."

He pointed to the growing damp area on the sheet. "For the moment, I'd like to keep our little arrangement confidential."

"Yes, Sir." I wondered what the day shift would make of the smell of sex that hovered in the room. I donned my bra and reached around for my panties, which lay crumpled on top of the sheet. Dr. Carver grabbed them before I could.

"I think I'll keep these," he said, stuffing them under his pillow.

"Whatever you wish, Sir."

"And from now on, Cassie, I want you to come to work without any underwear. It will make everything more convenient. No brassiere, no panties. And wear a skirt, not those silly inaccessible trousers."

"But, Sir..."

"Are you going to argue with me, slave?" His grin belied his cautionary tone.

I felt the gathering wetness soaking the crotch of my trousers. "Of course not, Sir. But I don't know if this kind of—activity—is good for a man in your condition."

"On the contrary. Anything that gives me the motivation to suffer through the endless hours of physical and occupational therapy that I'm facing is good, in my book." His smile was an affectionate challenge. "I'm determined to reach the point where I can flog you the way you deserve. You'd like that, wouldn't you?"

I hugged myself, amazed and delighted. "If it pleases you, Sir, then I'd like it very much."

SUNDAY IN THE STUDY

Justine Elyot

I never know how long he will make me wait.

Never less than five minutes, usually between ten and twenty, and on one unfondly recalled occasion, I was standing hands-on-head listening to the steady tick of the grandfather clock behind me for over an hour.

This, he says, is Reflection Time. I am to spend it thinking through any of the week's tribulations or missed opportunities, and considering how I will account for them. That is the theory, although in practice these tense minutes lend themselves to speculation. How many? How long? What will he use? Will I be able to sit at the family dinner afterward?

Later I will find myself in reflective mode once more, but this time I will be facing a corner, holding my hands clasped in the small of my back, above my bare and throbbing bottom. This is Recovery Time and usually lasts half an hour, long enough for tears to dry and sins to be absolved before we move into the final stage of the process: Forgiveness and Reconnection.

You will gather from all of this that Sinclair and I are lovers of ritual. What holds us together is something more than our mutual kink, our undeniable attraction and all the usual romantic folderol. It is our need for this Sunday to be like every other Sunday, in essence, even if certain elements are allowed to vary. It is my need for correction and his for control. When we were younger, my Sundays were spent in church, while he captained the school cricket team. As adults, we have exchanged these rituals for their deviant counterpart. He dominates, as he did his ten bowlers and batsmen; I submit, as I did to the God I worshipped. But this time there is nothing unpredictable, nothing unknowable, nothing to fear. It is all so much more satisfying.

Tick...*Perhaps the strap*...tock...*I hope not the cane*...tick... *But then again*...tock...*I like the cane*...tick...*I must be insane*...tock.

The door opens.

I know the drill. I remove my hands from my head and lower my eyes, letting my vision drift over the familiar pattern of the Persian runner, through the doorway and across the highly polished oak floorboards. My feet follow their gaze until they are stopped by the obstacle of his desk.

I love his desk. It is so antique it even has an inkwell. When I am bending over it, I can see my face in the mirror shine, though I tend to screw my eyes shut rather than watch my contorted expressions. Rarely, he requires me to keep them open—for instance, on the day that he invited his Dominatrix friend to watch and take notes. I had to look her in the eye through twenty-four strokes of the tawse, an almost impossible task, though I am proud to say I managed it to their satisfaction.

He walks, always in a slow, stately fashion, from the door to the desk. He stands on the other side of it, looking down at me with his more-in-sorrow-than-anger face for a moment.

"Well, Beth, here we are again," he says. "I wonder if the day will come when I do not have to waste my Sunday morning taking you to task over imperfections of behavior." We both know it will not. "No answer to that, hmm? Well, it does seem a very distant prospect to me, as well. Now then."

He seats himself and pulls over a large book, a leather-bound ledger. Large as it is, after two years it is already half filled with page after page of copperplate script, remembrances of crimes past and their associated sentences. He opens it, flipping the leaves to where the ribbon bookmark lies across a blank expanse.

Not blank for long though, for soon a fountain pen is slanted between his elegant fingers, dipped in the inkwell and put to the page. As he writes, he talks, his murmur following the looping progress of the pen.

"Sunday, June eighteenth," he says, then he holds the pen in suspended animation and looks at me. "What should I write, do you think? Any ideas?"

I never reply to this at first. Although the rules of our contract are perfectly clear, and he is unfailingly consistent in his enforcement of them, my mind blanks as soon as I enter the study and does not refill again until much later. Somewhere behind my shivering anticipation and survival techniques, I am aware that I smoked a cigarette, or left the television on standby, but it is all too distant for immediate retrieval.

"I...can't think, Sir," I admit.

"Come on, Beth—you were the one that used to confess to priests. Did your memory fail you then, too?"

"No. But five Hail Marys..." I trail off, reddening.

"Quite a different proposition to six strokes of the cane. Yes, I do see that."

Oh, god, not the cane. But I like the cane. But it hurts!

He sees the flicker in my eyes and chuckles slightly, his sadistic reflex flexing.

"Very well. I shall tally the scores." His pen begins to document the evidence of my transgressions, committing my guilt to permanent record. "On Monday, you left the house without charging your mobile phone, so you were unobtainable for the space of three hours. On Wednesday, you ate only three of your five daily portions of fruit and vegetables. Yesterday, you did not go swimming..."

He looks sharply up at me. I had no idea he knew this, and I have made an incoherent exclamation. "I..." I cannot lie though. "Oh," I say anticlimactically. "I just went to the shops instead. I didn't think...you would mind."

"I don't," he says. "I don't mind if you go shopping. I do mind if a friend of yours calls me from the pool to ask me why you haven't met her there as arranged and I can't account for it, though. You know our rules. One of them relates to honesty. And if you genuinely thought I wouldn't mind, why, then, did you not tell me at the time?"

Tough question. *Because I wanted to be found out,* flits through my head, but the rules of the game will not allow this kind of honesty. *We do it because it's hot,* is not the dynamic that arouses us at all. *We do it because it's hot but we pretend that we don't,* is much closer, though still only partly articulating the subtlety and complexity of our compact.

"I didn't think to," is what I actually say.

"I didn't think to, *Sir,*" he corrects me. My legs weaken and moisture seeps between them. I repeat the phrase. "I think we can categorize thoughtlessness under the heading of disrespect, Beth."

I bite my lip. Disrespect always means the cane.

He writes out my sentence, then signs it with his usual flourish and pushes the ledger across the desk for my perusal.

"Read it," he instructs.

"*Ten strokes of the number-two strap for general disobedience, followed by six strokes of the cane.*" This is never easy to say; my voice seems to blush as it reads. Sometimes he makes me repeat the words, but today he does not, which is one scrap of relief to hold close. I sign my name under his, my scrawl messy and disorganized beneath his perfectly reined-in script. He even has Dom handwriting.

"Good," he says briskly, glancing at the book before opening the Drawer of Pain. "We shall proceed. Over the desk, please, Beth."

I arrange myself carefully, hinged at the waist, my hands reaching to grasp the far rim of the desk, while he reaches into the drawer and withdraws just one of a vast range of nasty leather and wooden implements. This one is maroon leather, not the thickest nor the stiffest, but still capable of delivering a memorable sting. Ten strokes with it will warm and redden my bottom just sufficiently to prepare it for the cane.

Sinclair places the strap on the desk, rises and moves around behind me. I am wearing the light skirt and sheer white knickers he specified. He runs his hands over my jutting backside, rubbing at the whisper-thin cotton, pulling it taut and then letting it go slack before dealing two ringing smacks to each cheek.

"When will you learn, Beth," he asks, lifting the hem to my waist so that only my tight mesh knickers offer any posterior protection, "that I take disciplinary matters very seriously indeed? Hmm?"

My only response is a yelp as a volley of faster smacks hails onto the barely there fabric.

"After two years of Sundays spent over this desk, one would expect something to have sunk in," he says, peeling the knickers off my pinkening rump and letting them rest at midthigh. "And yet, here I am again, faced with the unenviable duty of visiting punishment on your recidivist bottom."' He sighs, a little over-theatrically, and I stifle a giggle. He does lay it on a mite too thick sometimes.

Amusement is soon replaced by clenching of muscles when he applies his hard, smooth hand to my bare bum, over and over and over until I can barely maintain my ignoble position. My breathy grunts cloud the perfect polish of the desk so that my nose tip is dampened, skidding around in time with the smacks. My fingers cling to the edge, but at the same time I must take care not to let my nails mark the surface. From this position it is difficult to focus on anything but the direction, speed and solidity of the next stroke, but somehow I have learned to keep a part of my mind concentrated on what Sinclair calls *appropriate behavior.*

No swearing. No badmouthing him. No kicking up with my feet or reaching behind to shield my bottom. I can plead all I like, but only the invocation of my safeword will make the slightest shred of difference.

None of this is unmanageable at first, but once the strap is flexed and flipped and brought to bear on my bottom, the alert level changes. I start to think about my breathing, I start to think about how many, mentally placing myself at the end of the ordeal before it begins. Always, about two or three strokes in, the question, *Why do I do this, why do I like this,* blares across my brain in panicking neon, but I know the answer well enough to take another bracing breath and push my stoic behind back out.

The strap falls with its primitively satisfying crack, over and over. It is stiff enough to penetrate to my muscle, flexible enough to sting a red stripe across my skin. I know why this is so—I oil them myself once a week. On a Saturday morning, I take a spray bottle containing one part white vinegar to three parts linseed oil and use it to keep Sinclair's straps and tawses and leather-covered paddles in the optimum condition for striping my backside. I spray on the mixture and rub it in with a soft microfiber cloth, then I soak the canes in a bucket of water to keep them pliable and whippy enough for Sir's purposes.

I certainly seem to have performed my task with admirable efficacy this week—the strap slaps down, painting its localized sunburn in a pattern of regular rectangles across the fleshiest section of my rump. I make it to ten, then relax, twitching across the desktop like a fish on dry land, moaning my relief.

His fingertips brush the heated flesh, assessing its temperature.

"Nicely warmed up," is the verdict. One finger ventures lower, into the depths, finding the lips swollen and sticky. "Hmm," he says, as he always does. "Lesson not learned yet, Beth?"

"Oh, yes, Sir, it is," I tell him, trying to split my sex on this one lean visitor, to enfold it and vacuum it up.

"Then, why...so...wet? Oh, no, I don't think we are finished here."

Ah, how cruelly he withdraws his foraging digit, moving around to the front of the desk and making me lick it clean.

"Stand up, Beth, and fetch me a cane. A nice thin one, I think."

Fetching the cane: a simple enough act, and yet one that can never be unthinkingly performed, for it requires such a fine pitch of submission. I am absolutely conscious of what I am doing when I stand and make my way neatly to the umbrella stand where the canes hang. I select one, nice and thin as requested, and picture the imprint it will make on my body. Even knowing what is in store for me, I make a steady journey back to Sinclair and hold my offering out to him in upturned palms.

"A good choice," he says, picking it up and flexing it to its utmost capacity. "This one marks so exquisitely." He holds it out in front of him, its slender length curtailed at each end by his knuckles. I know what is coming next. He raises it so that it is a whisper away from my lips. "Kiss the rod, Beth."

I graze my lips against the rattan. The air is heavy with expectation. Now I must say the words. The most difficult words in the language.

"Please punish me as I deserve, Sir." I almost always stumble over the word *punish*, which usually comes out sounding like *punch*—though he would never take me up on such a request, thankfully. Sometimes he asks me to speak up, or enunciate more clearly. Today is such a day.

"Please...what?" he asks, tilting his head down toward me.

I bite my lip and regain my breath. "Punish me," I mutter.

"Punish you? Is that what you want?"

"Yes, Sir."

"Good. Because I intend to punish you, Beth. Now let's have you back over the desk, please."

Questioning my sanity as ever, I drape myself back into position. I am still aglow from the effects of hand and strap, and I half wish I could see my bottom in a mirror. One thing I constantly regret is not being able to watch my flesh coloring and jiggling and acquiring those cruel but lovely patterns Sinclair delights in creating. Perhaps I can prevail on him to film us one day. Until then...

I must content myself with the sounds, with the shivers, with the buildup. He swooshes the cane through the air at my hind, then he taps it gently across my bottom in a series, then he lays it flat where my buttocks swell broadest. I am never prepared for this. I know that it will be painful and hateful, but I know that the pain and hate will be worthwhile, and that, give or take a day for the marks to stop pulsing, I will want to do it all over again.

The fearful swish comes faster than I expected; I am caught off guard by the slice of white heat and I scream, jumping up and letting go of the desk. My hands almost forget the rule and flit back to cover my vulnerable bum—a crime that would earn me at least two more strokes—but I recover my position just in time.

"Don't tell me you weren't expecting that," says Sinclair, sadistically amused. "Are you struck dumb?"

"No, Sir. One, Sir." The count is an essential part of the business, cruelly forcing my mind to stay in its present instead of drifting off to safer places. If form is anything to go by, the next stroke will land just half an inch or so below the first. I shut my eyes and visualize its impact, the whiteness then the redness as a line of roused blood rushes to the surface. Somehow this helps.

With each stroke I contemplate the use of my safeword, yet I am certain I will not say it. Although we do this every Sunday without fail, Sinclair is always so mindful of my prevailing emotional weather that if he knows I am not up to the full force of the law, he will do something else, such as put me over his knee, and his voice will be softer, his lectures gentler, his hand still sharp but only in the knowledge that we both want that glow at the end of the process. If I were not in the right frame of mind for the cane, I would not be bent over this desk, here, now, bottom aflame, lip chewed to raggedness, waiting and hoping for more.

The sixth, as ever, almost breaks me, and my knees buckle while the varnished wood muffles my scream. It burns at the base of my buttocks, radiating heat downward to my thighs, sitting in exactly the right spot to ensure discomfort for a day or two at least.

"Six, Sir." Ah, I want so much to rub, to touch, to feel the heat, but I am forbidden and, after all, I will be disappointed if it fades too quickly, so I am obedient, maintaining my bent stance until I am permitted to rise.

"Good," says Sinclair. "I will accept your thanks now, Beth."

I rise, wiping chaotic stray hair from my face, which feels crumpled and hot. It takes me a little while to recover my breath and properly compose myself, but when I have, I turn to face him. His expression afterward is one of the sweetest thrills of the experience, though I still long to be able to see his face as he lays his strokes; it often appears in my fantasies. He still looks stern, but there is a gleam and a flush of pleasurable exertion; his impeccable hair might be slightly disheveled and his long fingers fidget with the cane.

I look him straight in the eye and say, "Thank you, Sir, for giving me what I need and deserve." I have said it so often now that the words come easily, but they are never glib—my attention can never skid sideways and pretend I am saying something less mortifying. He would not allow that.

"You are most welcome." He takes my elbow and leads me to the large mirror on the back wall, showing me the view he plans to enjoy for the next half hour—red stripes on pink, palpable soreness. Then he tucks my skirt firmly into its waistband and makes me walk, awkwardly given that my knickers are still around my knees, to the designated corner.

I stand there for half an hour, holding the cane behind my back as a reminder, feeling the warmth march on and on, far beyond the borders of my punishment area, down to my weak knees, up to my stony nipples, across to my seeping slit. I want him now, want him wildly, yet he sits at his desk, rustling his newspaper, answering phone calls, watching me burn for him. Here is the real cruelty.

When the clock releases me, the mood will change. There will be kisses, there will be touching, there may be nuzzling and suckling, there may be fingering and licking, and eventually there will certainly be more bending over, accompanied by the spreading of legs and lips or even bottom cheeks. There will be a reestablishment of connection, a return to affectionate terms, and all will be well again.

But at the family dinner afterward, I will perch precariously on my seat, wishing I could ask for a cushion without occasioning unwanted interest. I will feel the swollen stripes when I bathe or shower, when I pull up my knickers, when I lie in bed, when I drive to work, when I walk wearing jeans or a tight skirt. And when I stop feeling them, then my mind will turn to next Sunday, and what it might hold in store for me.

WALKING THE SUB

Salome Wilde

What could be nicer on a warm sunny day than having your dear Master take you for a walk in the park? He'd been solicitous and generous one bright May morning, after having put me through a particularly grueling session (with the manacles and black leather belt I've come to know and love) the night before. I had the day off and he was playing hooky from work. He put me in the shower and soaped and lathered me, tasted my sweet clean pussy, then toweled me dry, brushed my silky black hair and put it up into a ponytail the way he likes it. All the while, he kept a serious, purposeful face, doing a job and doing it well. Those blue eyes just melted me, as always, as he worked.

He had me dress him in boxers, nice-fitting jeans, white T-shirt that shows off his pecs, socks, athletic shoes. I waited for him to choose clothes for me, but he just scooted me out of my room with a smile on his face and a collar in his hand. He collared and leashed me with the soft, pale blue leather accouterments we both adore, strapped on my comfy walking sandals, then tossed his oversized button-down shirt around my shoulders. Helping me slip my arms through, rolling the cuffs, and doing up a couple of buttons, he held my gaze and spoke, a telltale hint of excitement in his voice: "You've been such a good girl lately, I have a little treat planned for us."

I wanted to glance down at his jeans to see how good this "treat" was going to be. The hardness of his cock as he thought about what we'd do was a very reliable meter. But that wasn't part of the game. I had to keep my eyes on his, and it wasn't hard: his even white teeth gleamed at me through a grin that said he knew I wanted to see that bulge in his jeans but was winning the battle to be perfectly obedient. He reached both hands down to pull gently on my nipples and watched my eyes. They clouded with desire. He pulled harder. I moaned. He stopped.

"Good girl. Now come along." And he tugged on the leash and drew me along behind. "Come along" indeed: with my sweet, sexy Master holding the chain, how could I do anything else? And why would I, even if I could? But he must have noticed some hesitation in me, given that he was heading out the door and I was wearing only a thin shirt that exposed most of me. He turned to face me again. "Trust me, pet."

I smiled up at him.

"And obey me." He swatted me hard on the ass and turned again to go. I swallowed hard and followed, determined to live up to this D/s dare. We went out through the back door and walked to the garage. He paused and pointed to the newspaper at his feet in the driveway. A car whizzed by. Being in a particularly obedient and playful mood, I bent completely over, knees straight, letting the soft shirt slide up to display my sweet little ass. He swore softly. He loves my ass. He moved behind me, grabbed my hips, and ground the rough denim of his jeans into my backside, letting me feel how hard he was for me. I won-

dered if my juices would coat his fly. I moaned softly, hugging my
ankles. He moved back a bit, then slipped a finger into me. He
pumped it slowly, rubbing it all around inside me. I knew what
that meant, and held my breath. He withdrew it, then slipped it
fast and hard into my ass. I gasped. I knew he must be smiling
behind me. Each time he did that, I tried my best not to gasp. It
was part of my training, but I hadn't gotten that sudden intake
of breath controlled yet. I heard him laugh gently. "It's okay, pet.
I like that my touch excites you." He shoved his finger in deeper,
began to drive it into me, his other hand on my hip. "More?"

I nodded and he pressed another finger in beside the first.
I was tight, especially so in this position. And I was nervous,
knowing other cars could drive by any moment. Even though it
was a quiet street, and even though what he was doing wasn't
entirely obvious, my ass was still naked and hiked up in the air.
So his fingers inside me were an especially strong combination
of pain and pleasure, and I basked in my own nervousness, mild
discomfort, and delight.

"You'd like me to take my cock out right now and fuck you
with it, wouldn't you, my sweet little slut?" he asked as he drove
his fingers in and out. "I can see how wet you are, pet. So hungry for your Master's thick, hard cock." I whimpered, moved
my hands from ankles to asphalt, arched harder into his fingers.
"Yes, that's right, slut. Take it deeper." He shoved them more
roughly into me. "I love your tight asshole, slut," he groaned. "I
could fuck you like this all day."

I murmured, "Yes...yes...fuck me," until he stopped suddenly. And I knew, without a doubt, that he'd stopped when
he knew I was enjoying myself. He kept control of me with
constant teasing, arousing, mild punishment, and other uses. I
breathed hard, remaining bent over, with his hand on the small
of my back.

"My paper, pet," he said, calmly.

I opened my eyes and looked down at the newspaper in its little plastic sleeve. To offer him extra pleasure, I bent my elbows and stretched farther down and forward, exposing what I hoped was an even better shot of my ass and soaked pussy, and grabbed the paper with my teeth. Walking my hands back, I bent my knees and sat down on my haunches, tugging a bit at the leash, then turning and looking up at my Master with hands at my sides and his paper in my mouth. He ruffled my hair and took the paper, smiling brightly. "Good girl," he laughed. "Obedient and talented." A car zoomed by, and I was glad I was reasonably well covered by the shirt as I sat.

He tugged me up and walked me back to the door of the garage, then inside. "Taking your good dog for a drive, Sir?" I asked, smiling.

He yanked hard on the leash. He pulled my face close to his. The smile was gone from his eyes. "I'm doing with you what I desire. Whatever I desire. And you will not question this. Do you understand, girl?"

"I understand, Sir," I said in the steady voice expected of me at such times, meeting his eyes dutifully. So much for play.

But his gaze softened at my obedience, and he let the leash slacken. He quickly surprised me again, however, when he opened the back rather than the front passenger door for me and motioned me inside. I did not question, but hopped in, sitting comfortably in the plush backseat, looking up at him. "Fold your legs under and sit like a nice pet," he said firmly, and watched as I did so. Next, he fastened my leash to the hook for hanging clothes above the window. As I followed his actions with my eyes, I knew it would be simple to unhook the leash, so this was clearly about psychological submission, not physical.

"Lick me, girl," he said with a smile, offering the back of

his palm. I bent my head and licked. "Good girl. You love your Master, don't you?" He tousled my hair. "Now give me a kiss, honey," he oozed in that voice reserved for the family pet, bringing his face close to mine. I pressed a slightly opened mouth to his to kiss him. He pulled away sharply and brought his hand down to slap my thigh, hard. "Bad girl!" he snapped. "Don't put that muzzle on my mouth!" I understood. I nodded, my thigh stinging and the trace of a handprint beginning to show. I put my hands between my knees and locked my elbows, then held my head up and stuck out my tongue. "Yes, pet," he drawled, and offered his cheek. I lapped at it twice. He smiled and stroked my back. "That's my good, good girl." He backed out and closed the door.

And I was taken, entirely like the family dog, for a ride.

We headed quickly out of town and into the country. He opened my window halfway, and I fed his desire for my petlike obedience by putting my head out and letting the breeze whip my ponytail behind me. He glanced in the rearview mirror and grinned. "Who's my good girl?" he cooed. I answered with a little yelp, which widened his smile further. This puppy knew how to please her Master. But I gave him an even bigger thrill when a red pickup with a burly, bearded redneck drove up beside us. I smiled brightly at him and flashed a bit of tit, then, as he slowed to see more, I saw the dog in the back and barked at it. The dog seemed more puzzled than the man (who was distracted by my 36Ds), but joined the barking game, and soon we were a wild duo. My delighted Master turned his head halfway around and, between laughs, yelled, "Down, girl! Stop that! Bad! Bad girl!" I kept it up, the big black lab pacing, wagging his tail, and yapping back at me. I tried to do the same, pulling against the leash to crawl agitatedly around the backseat, then returned to the window to yelp some more. As my enchanted Owner shook his

head and chuckled, the pickup put on speed and breezed past
us—to get away from the "crazy woman," no doubt.

Giddy with my own performance, I put my "paws" up and
licked the hand that lay across the back of the passenger seat.
Without turning, he stroked my hair. I could see his still-enor-
mous grin through the rearview mirror. "Such a devoted pet,"
he murmured. "Let's see if we can't reward such a good little
thing." He flicked on the turn signal and we exited the main
road and headed to Mona Park, a small recreational area and
boat dock we'd driven past dozens of times but never visited before. When we parked, he turned around and put my face in his
hands. My lips parted of their own accord. "You're gonna love
this, baby," he breathed hotly, an inch from my mouth. I wanted
the kiss that hovered between us, badly, but he didn't offer it.
Before he could pull away, I licked his cheek. "Moist little beast,
aren't you?" he said, smirking. I could feel wetness trickle down
between my legs.

The park was nearly deserted, and I was grateful for it as
my sweet Master opened the car door and escorted me out, still
leashed and standing tall. I felt my cheeks redden and warm
as my shirttails fluttered in a breeze that exposed and tingled
my pussy. He watched my face, devouring my blush with pleasure, then glanced down. He brushed his fingers across the little
shaved triangle above my labia, then swatted it playfully. He
loved that little trimmed tuft, loved to tease and tug on it. He
slipped a finger quickly inside my clean-shaven folds, making
me gasp, then he pulled it out and sucked on it. I watched his
lips take in his finger, saw his cheeks draw in around it. He
hummed in his throat, tasting my sweet spiciness. I moaned
softly, my eyes drifting shut, waiting for more. He tugged lightly
on my leash, making me open and bring my eyes level with his;
then he reached down again and plumbed my depths, grinding

his fingers deep into me, stroking up across my clit with each of five deft plunges. I was deeply aroused and more than a little nervous, wondering if anyone was close enough to see us. But I held his gaze. I groaned as he stopped then brought his fingers to my lips, painting my pout with sticky wetness.

He watched himself work my mouth gently open. I adored the intensity of his gaze as he parted his lips along with mine. He was in control, but he was so hungry for me. The subtlety of the way power works in such a situation is more than magical; it is utterly intoxicating. "That's right, baby," he sighed, pressing warm juicy fingers onto my tongue. I knew not to suck. First of all, when he played this way I was to remain passive, let him tell me what to do and when. Second, I was his pet today. I didn't want to break the spell. He slid his fingers back and forth over my tongue, enjoying my stillness.

The look in his eyes suddenly shifted, and I knew he need-ed to take more active control. What a delight to watch him swing that way. "Lick them clean, girl," he said, without emo-tion. "Take care of your Master." I lapped softly, tasting myself warm and sharp on his fingers. "That's right." He spread them so I could lick between, then pulled up on my leash and began to walk with me. I was a single pace behind, my pussy leaking more moisture as I anticipated pleasure and knew it would be risky and challenging. I was glad I was far from town and would likely know no one here if caught.

He, of course, knew I'd be nervous, and I was thrilled when he aimed us into the shelter of the forest. He led me awhile along a trail, quietly. When we stopped and he looked around, I leaned forward to lick his neck. "Excited, girl?" he said, turn-ing to face me. I smiled and licked again. "Well, come on then, let's get comfy." He walked us to a bench beside the trail. I went to sit down beside him. "Bad girl!" he snapped, yanking my leash. I brought my hands to my collar. "Put your hands down," he said. "Don't tug at that collar or I'll have to tie your wrists." I wanted my hands free, so I obeyed. He sat down on the bench as I stood, leaving a little slack in my leash. I was grateful, and waited for him to speak or act. He rubbed the soft leather loop at the end of the leash with his thumb. While he stroked back and forth, I watched his small gesture, patiently, until he spoke again.

"Turn around," he said, plainly. I did so. "Bend forward." I looked both ways for walkers, then bent over and arched my ass up for his pleasure. He snapped the leash end across my ass, hard. I yelped and winced. It stung. He struck again. Then a third time. "That," he said, "is for looking around before you obeyed me. Now, let us get to the punishment for presuming to sit beside me rather than at my feet, like a good little animal." I shivered; I knew my ass was reddening and that he was enjoying it. I could not see him, bent forward with hands above my knees as I was. But I knew he was rising, and I knew my ass was in trouble. His hand came down with a loud smack that sent some forest creatures skittering noisily away. I managed not to cringe as he hit me three more times, but it brought tears to my eyes. He spanked me once more with both hands, and I held still and kept silent. "Good girl," he said, a smile in his voice. "Now back up and bring that poor little red ass to your Master." I stayed bent forward and took a step back. I closed my eyes and waited. I loved this part. He reached forward and held my hips, then dragged his soft, warm, wet tongue over my cheeks. Three licks, four, five, cool air soothing me with each broad lap. "Better?" he asked when he'd finished. I nodded heavily, so he could see. "Very nice, pet. Now sit where you're supposed to."

I turned around, then knelt beside him, resting my ass

lightly on my heels. The ground was uneven and strewn with pebbles and twigs. I adjusted myself as comfortably as I could. The small pain served as further silent penitence. He caressed my hair and looked around. "Beautiful day, girl. Just beautiful. Smell those flowers. What could be better than a day out, walking my sub." He laughed. I smiled, leaned my face on his lap. "Such a good girl. I think you deserve a little treat, don't you?" I nodded, face still resting on his thighs. "Sit up now. That's it." I sat up, nice and tall, waiting for him to offer me his cock. I was overjoyed when that is exactly what he did. He unzipped his fly and released his nice thick hard-on, then moved his hands away. I reached out for it, but he slapped my hand away. "No!" he scolded. "Don't touch Master's treasure with your dirty little paws."

I nodded. I understood. I bent forward and pushed out my tongue to lap at his delicious hard cock. Within a few strokes, he was leaking precome that I devoured greedily, delighted at having earned it so quickly. My dear Master murmured softly in his throat, again stroking my hair with one hand while his other held the leash loosely. I dipped deeper and pressed my nose into his balls so I could lick beneath. He arched his hips and wriggled his pants down a bit farther to give me access. I loved how much he wanted my mouth on him. I licked and lapped at him, nuzzling in and teasing his asshole with the tip of my tongue. He moaned. I wanted those pants off; I reached up a hand.

He sat up sharply. He grabbed my wrist. "Damn it, girl, didn't you hear me? No paws." He shook his head at me, wrapped his hand around most of the leash and tugged hard to bring my face to his groin. "I guess you need me to show you." He wound his free hand around my ponytail, gripping it where it met my head, and pushed me down on his cock. I took it in as deep as I could, trying not to gag. "Suck it." I did so, my leash keeping me from moving, his hand pulling my hair to set the pace he desired. He groaned as I swirled my tongue around his shaft when he allowed me breathing room. I moved up and down the length of him, just the way he liked. My throat relaxed as I accepted his control. Moisture pooled between my legs as I felt him swell in my mouth. He neared climax far more quickly than I knew he'd like, and I basked in it, pouring all of my desire and need to give myself to him into the way I sucked his hard cock. After a few more strokes, he pulled me sharply off him, brought my lips to his for a deep, plundering kiss. I moaned in my throat as he devoured my mouth, stroking my tongue roughly with his. I felt my insides turn to molten lava as my pussy clenched and released.

As if he knew, he reached for me. "Sit up, girl." I got to my knees. He unbuttoned my shirt and pushed it back to fall from my shoulders. The breeze was heaven, but I was so worried someone would walk by. I didn't dare let the nervousness show on my face, however, or he might stop. He admired me, sitting there, the sun through the trees speckling me with shadows. "My sweet little dalmatian," he said, tracing the "spots" on my shoulders with gentle fingertips. He let his touch dance over my skin, down to my breasts, then released my leash (so trusting), to caress and knead my breasts. "Sweet, sweet girl," he whispered, filling his hands with me. My eyelids drifted shut, until I felt the sharp pain of my nipples being pulled up hard. "Did I tell you to close your eyes?" I shook my head, eyes meeting his. He pulled harder. I struggled not to wince. My pussy, ever the betrayer, offered a thin trail of sap down the inside of my right thigh. I shuddered.

My observant Master didn't miss that little trail. He released my nipples and came to stand behind me, leash once again in hand. He pushed my legs apart, then came down to my level. I sighed as he pressed his warm, clothed body up against mine. He took two fingers and swept them along the track of wetness down my leg, then brought his fingers to his lips and sucked them loudly. "Mine for the taking, aren't you, sweet baby?" As he spoke, he reached between my legs, pressed his cock there, and rubbed against my slit. I let my head drop back, moaning softly. "Oh, yes, sweet little pussy...all mine to use. So sweet..." I knew he was far gone when he talked a string like this, repeating "sweet" in every phrase. He wanted me, and he would have me, any way he chose.

With a swift, fluid motion, he pressed forward and had the head of his cock inside me before I knew it. He ground in small circles and held me still, hands digging into my hips. I moaned. With a growl that thrilled me to my hungry core, he plunged in, hilting himself within me as his balls slapped against my clit. I cried out and my ass received a slap for my lack of control. "Quiet, my ravenous little bitch," he ground out, holding himself still. He was tense. He wanted to let go, I knew, but not until he had the submission he sought from me. He never called me "bitch"—but it worked so well now, as he took me, doggy-style, his greedy little pet in heat. My breathing was quick and hard; I tried to calm it, to slow it, to make myself quiet and tranquil for him. He began to ride me again, fully in control now, with long deep strokes that kept my pulse racing and my pussy soaked. He pumped faster, fingers gripping my hips hard, balls rhythmically spanking my lips and clit, rough thighs slapping into the soft backs of mine. I began to press back into him, to meet his rhythm. "No. Be still, bitch," he snapped, and continued his assault, reaching up to slip a thumb into my pussy beside his cock, then, nicely slicked, into my ass. "Take what your Master gives...feel my need and be...satisfied...in giving yourself up to my will..."

I loved when he got so hot that he talked this way: power mad and in stuttered phrases, controlled yet wild. I nearly swooned with it and the relentless grind into my sodden cunt and tight ass. Then, he arched over me and grabbed my hair, fucking me like we were both animals, he a greedy predator, I his eager prey. He drove into me, for minutes or hours, until we were both sweating as he strained to reach his climax and I my own. Each thrust brought him closer, his cock swelling inside me. His balls kept a steady beat on my clit and his hand tugged at my hair to bring me over, shattering around him, my mind swirling, body arching, a gasp then a hoarse cry pouring from my throat as my muscles locked of their own accord. My contractions milked his climax from him, drove him over the edge with a groan of hunger so deep it was hard to tell if he felt pleasure or pain. But I smiled as he shook my body with his orgasm, coming deep and hot within me, then more over my pussy and ass as he pulled out.

"Oh, sweet baby," he muttered, "sweet fucking angel cunt." I smiled at his string of orgasm-induced epithets, enjoying every moment of his exultation. "Damn, that pussy drives me wild." He brought his mouth down and licked and sucked our mingled juices. I basked in the gentle attention until he sank back onto his heels. I turned around and sat, too, smiling up at him. He leaned forward and pressed a brief kiss to my lips, both of us breathing too hard yet to do more. He smiled and brushed a hand down my back. He stopped suddenly, the Master back fully in his eyes. "Oh, shit, girl, look at this mess." His hand was covered with come. "Clean this, pet, right now." I leaned forward and lapped at it, licking up the thick, cool, musky liquid that clung to his fingers. I hated cold come but nothing would prevent me from obeying this order. When he was clean enough, he stood and wiped his hands on his pants, then did up his fly.

"All right, come on, girl; we have to get you cleaned up, too." I
rose, and he took hold of my leash again. He began to walk.

"Hey, wait," I said, laughing. "I don't have any clothes on."
He yanked on the leash. "Stop that growling, right now.
You know you need a bath, girl, and you're going to get one." I
looked up, astonished. Surely he wouldn't...

But he did. He walked us straight toward the fishermen at
the edge of the lake. I shook my head, pulled against the leash.
"Bad girl!" he shouted, turning to spank my ass hard. "Heel!"

I felt dared. And I was up to any dare he could come up
with—especially as none of the guys fishing looked even slightly
familiar. So I walked, obediently, a pace behind him, the leash
now slack but still in my Master's hand. I smiled brightly at one
of the fishermen. He did a double take right out of a slapstick
comedy. All three of them stared, slack-jawed.

"Stay, girl," my Master said, leaving me for a moment while
he bent to pick something up. I obeyed, eyes watching him. He
grabbed a stick. I grinned, shook my head. "Gotta get you to
take a bath somehow, pet. Now fetch!" He unhooked my leash
and threw the stick into the water. I stared at him a moment,
waiting to be sure he was truly serious about this. "Go on, girl!"
he gushed. I headed in, running then swimming out to get it.
The water was cold and tightened my nipples. I swam hard to
get used to it, then grabbed the stick in my hand before placing
it between my teeth. I turned and paddled back, enjoying the
enormous grin on my Master's face that turned into delighted laughter. The fishermen were mumbling to themselves, one
smiling, one shaking his head, and the other still silent with his
mouth hanging open. My thoughtful Master held out my shirt
for me as I walked ashore, soaking wet. A bit out of breath, I
approached quietly, humbly. I walked tall, pretending to ignore
the others' gazes, then I dropped the stick at Master's feet. He

smiled and leaned forward to kiss me. I took a step back and, with all my might, shook my head and body to splash him head to toe with cold lake water.

He gasped. I grabbed the shirt and ran before he could get hold of my leash. I raced him to the car, knowing he'd catch me before I could get inside. He pursued, reaching for the leather dangling from my neck. "Oh, you're gonna get it, girl!" he threatened, laughter in his voice. I got to the car first, but, of course, he had locked the doors and had the keys. I turned to see him slowly approaching, dangling the keychain from his fingertip. "Need something, pet?" His dirty little smile promised much, and the bulge in his jeans promised even more. I smiled and licked my lips, giddy with desire to find out what punishment he'd think up when he got me into that backseat.

JUST WHAT
SHE NEEDS

Donna George Storey

What I needed that night was pasta.

Or rather, my boyfriend, Greg, needed pasta. I was supposed to stop at Raffetto's on my way home and get some fresh *linguine fini*. But I'd had a hell of a day with back-to-back depositions, and I forgot. Okay, I didn't actually forget, but I figured for once Mr. Gourmet could make do with some of the packaged stuff.

Suffice to say I wasn't in a very good mood when I walked in the door. However, the sight of curly-headed Greg at the stove stirring up *puttanesca* sauce with his big, capable hands definitely raised my spirits. The scent of good virgin olive oil, garlic and olives filled the kitchen and my mouth began to water. Greg was a web designer and worked at home, leaving him plenty of time to clean and cook and pamper me. I pretty much had me the ideal wife—with a big, juicy cock attached. Sometimes I felt so lucky to have him, I had to pinch myself.

But tonight, I just felt tired and annoyed.

"Today was an absolute nightmare," I greeted him, throwing down my briefcase on the bench inside the door and dumping my coat in a heap on top.

"That's too bad, sweetie. But now you can relax. Dinner's almost ready," Greg said, giving me a kiss and a glass of Chianti. "I just need to cook up the linguine."

"I didn't get it."

He frowned as if he didn't quite get it himself.

"Can't you use something from a box tonight? I mean pasta is pasta."

"Pasta is *not* pasta. You know that."

I rolled my eyes and reached into the cabinet for a package of spaghetti I'd bought before Greg moved in. "See, it says right here, this is Italy's best-selling brand. What's good enough for the Italians is good enough for us."

Greg gave me a patient smile. "Okay, I know you've had a hard day. I'll go buy it myself. You can start on the salad while I'm out. Some good food will make you feel better."

He was right, but like I said, I was in a bitchy mood, so his understanding only made me madder. "Why does dinner always have to be such a fucking big deal?" I grumbled. "I'm not even really hungry. I'll just have a yogurt." I reached for the refrigerator door.

That's when he said it, his voice so soft I could barely hear the words.

I know just what she needs.

My stomach did a somersault, and my arm flopped to my side like a rag doll's. Another five seconds passed before I remembered to breathe. When I finally exhaled, it came out as a soft whimper.

And my crotch was soaking wet.

I turned and glanced up at Greg. He wasn't smiling anymore.

"You know just what you need, Karen, don't you?"
There was a lump in my throat the size of a walnut. All I could manage was a nod.
"I want you to go take your shower. But first hang up your coat. You know you shouldn't leave it crumpled on the bench like that." Again his words were low and soft, a dead monotone. Yet the voice seemed to reach up inside me and give my secret muscles a deliciously painful squeeze. In fact, my whole body already felt sore, worked over, memory and anticipation twisted together so tightly I felt drunk. I walked over to the door, unsteadily, as if making my way through ankle-deep mud. Hands shaking, I eased my coat onto the rack and glanced over at him, awaiting my next command.
Greg was watching me, eyes narrowed.
"I can sense the attitude change already," he said. "Go get ready, I'll be with you in a few minutes."
I headed down the hall slowly, half hoping he might change his mind, call me back for a soothing hug instead.
Not that he ever did.
As I hung my skirt in the closet and tossed my blouse and underwear in the laundry basket, I heard pots rattling and water running out in the kitchen, ordinary sounds filtered through layers of thick gauze. But the ordinary world was already far behind me. With each step, each motion, thought slipped away, leaving only that sweet throbbing ache low between my legs.
Soon I would be in the place where I always got just what I needed.
I stepped into the bathroom and turned on the shower. Greg insisted that the water be as hot as I could take it. Wincing, I quickly soaped under my arms, between my legs, and circled my anus with a frothy finger. I held my buttcheeks open to the boiling spray, then turned and tilted my hips up to wash my labia. It

stung, as if a whole layer of skin had been seared away, but my soft, pink parts still plumped up in the heat, until my body was limp, feverish, tingling.

Drying off quickly, I grabbed an extra towel from the shelf. When I opened the door, Greg was already lounging on the bed in his bathrobe, stroking his erection idly through the terry cloth. His eyes flickered as they glided up and down my flushed body. Holding my gaze, he parted his robe to taunt me with the sight of his hard-on. He wrapped his fist around it and began to pump. His cock strained and swelled, the ruddy hue deepening to an angry red.

I felt another pang in my belly. He looked so big, and my tender places were already sore. I wasn't sure I could handle him today. But in the next instant that familiar flame sprang to life again in my groin.

He was going to give me just what I needed.

"Don't just stand there staring at my dick, Karen. You know what comes next."

I nodded, but the truth was I didn't. He changed the rules every time. Still, the opening ritual was pretty much the same. I walked over to the bed and placed the towel beside him.

Greg stopped stroking himself and crossed his hands behind his head, the picture of lordly leisure. His penis twitched. "Now get the goody bag."

By now the throbbing ache in my lower regions was almost making me sick to my stomach. I shuffled to the dresser and bent over to open the bottom drawer. I could feel Greg's eyes on my open cleft, still raw from the punishing spray of the shower. It suddenly struck me as odd then that we kept the bag of toys hidden away behind his workout clothes—as if some disapproving parent might find it and scold us for our perversions.

I pulled out the toiletries case, a cute thing made of padded paisley cotton. Today my "goody bag" felt somehow heavier and bulkier. Sometimes Greg bought a new gift—not to say torture device—at the sex-toy store on Seventh Avenue as a surprise.

I placed the bag on the nightstand beside him.

"Open it and lay everything on the table."

My hand shook as I unzipped the bag and reached inside. The first items were my oldest friends: a bottle of lube and an accordion of condom packets.

The next objects brought another sharp twinge of visceral memory. They were booty bumpers, or as Greg dubbed them, "The Three Bears." Goldilocks's buddies consisted of a set of silicone cocks with flared bases and helmeted heads. The smallest was pink and veered slightly to the left. The medium one was red and thicker; the last, six inches long and a troll-like green. I set them out in ascending order of size, glancing quickly at Greg for any sign of disapproval. He merely watched, a smile playing over his lips.

Next came a few latex gloves, a vibrating silver egg and a strand of purple silicone beads. Tucked at the bottom was indeed a new mystery item, a curved, rigid shape wrapped in vulva pink tissue. I felt a stab of fear mixed with curiosity. It seemed too small to be anything overly demanding, but Greg had a way of surprising me.

"Should I open the package?" I asked.

"Not yet," Greg said. "Just put it on the table."

I did as he ordered, then waited, hands at my sides, eyes trained on the carpet.

Greg exhaled audibly, with the patience of an exasperated schoolmaster. "You know your behavior down there was unacceptable."

"I know," I whispered.

"What do you need when you've been such a bad girl?"

My lips felt impossibly swollen and achy—just like the ones between my legs. "I need..." I faltered.

"Yes? Speak up."

"I...need to be fucked up the ass." The voice came out strange—not mine, a strangled, desperate sound.

"Really? Is that what you need?"

My eyes still fixed on the floor, I nodded.

"Is that what you want?"

I nodded.

"Then say it again nice and loud."

"I need...and I want...to be fucked up the ass." My shamefully obscene confession echoed through the bedroom, and I felt my whole body blush.

"Good girl. You may open your present."

My hands still trembled as I picked up the pink package. The paper tore easily to reveal a new butt plug for my growing collection. It was thicker than the others and curved in a way I recognized was meant to stimulate the G-spot. The silvery glitter embedded in the silicone reminded me of a festive occasion, like New Year's Eve.

"It's pretty." The words slipped out before I could stop myself.

"Is it?" Greg was studying my face with that same cool expression. "Do you think you'll like it as much when I shove it up your asshole?"

I swallowed.

"Well?"

"No, I...I think I'll like it more."

He laughed softly, a villain's chuckle. "I guess we'll find out soon enough. Spread out the towel and lie down."

I complied, dutifully lying back against the pillows, the towel under my buttocks.

Greg wrenched open my thighs and bent to study me. His tongue made a clicking sound.

"I should just fuck your ass right away, but I'm hungry. A smart-mouthed little bitch interrupted my dinner with her need to be punished. So I'm going to eat your pussy first. And you'd better do your best to get turned on because this is the only time I'm even gonna get within a mile of your clit. Understood?"

"Understood," I breathed.

"Oh, I forgot your new friend." Greg reached for the butt plug and paused to gaze at it with a fond smile. "Lucky little devil, going on in ahead of me."

Still smiling he inserted it up to the base in my vagina, then pulled it out again.

"This should do for lube. You're awfully wet. Tilt up a bit."

I lifted my buttocks a few inches off the bed. With a look of concentration, Greg teased my anus with the knob of the toy, circling, stroking, poking gently at the opening. The first few times he "punished" me, I tensed up, but now my asshole only needed just the slightest flirtation to open itself like a flower.

He pushed the toy inside me to the hilt.

I whimpered.

"Well?"

"It's different. There's a new pressure inside...it's good."

Greg nodded and positioned himself between my legs. "While I lick your clit, I want you to bear down on your new butt buddy. I want you to feel it deep inside and think of my cock. Understood?"

"Yes," I murmured.

He bent forward and touched my clit with the tip of his tongue. I sighed and quivered. On our first date, Greg told me his hobby was eating, and I wondered if the sly twinkle in his eye was a promise of other pleasures.

I soon discovered the guy was a champion pussy-licker. A year later he had a whole catalog of tricks to get me squirming. In no time my cunt was drooling, the juices dribbling down to coat the base of the plug, pooling on the towel beneath my ass.

I milked the toy with my ass muscles, imagining his thick cock inside me, just as he'd commanded. That long, thick tool was ready to fill my dirtiest hole with sweet, white cream. I moaned and squeezed harder. Each contraction brought me closer to orgasm, a road I'd embarked on the moment he'd murmured those magic words: *I know just what she needs.*

"I need it now," I blurted out.

Greg looked up at me, his lips shimmering with gloss. "What do you need, Karen?"

"I need your big, fat cock in my ass."

"Yes, I think you do," he murmured, rising up on his knees and reaching for the condoms.

I lay there watching, my juices still trickling down my slit in anticipation. Sometimes when he was lubed up, Greg merely pushed my knees up and took me on my back. Other times he made me straddle him and skewered my anus that way. But today he just narrowed his eyes and said, "Get on all fours like the little bitch you are."

Heart pounding, I scrambled into doggie position, careful to keep clutching the toy so it wouldn't pop out. Greg knelt behind me and rested his hand on my hip, a proprietary gesture, yet oddly comforting.

I waited, shivering.

When he pulled the toy out, my flesh made a soft kissing sound.

My breath was coming so fast, I thought I might faint. I felt so empty now, open and hungry. But finally I was going to get just what I needed.

Greg nudged the head of his cock against my opening, a gentle *knock, knock*. My muscles were so stretched and relaxed from the toy, I opened like an automatic door. He eased himself in, inch by inch.

We both sighed.

I started to move, the sensation radiating out from the ring of muscle to my skull, my toes. Each stroke sent fingers of pleasure tingling down my spine, like a virtuoso pianist at his keyboard. I could hardly believe it had only been six months since Greg took my virginity back there. Yet each time the feeling was more exquisite.

Again he reached toward the nightstand. Through the fog of my arousal, I heard the sound of low buzzing. Greg held the vibrating egg to my clit and I jumped. Flames licked my flesh, from clit to ass. Greg controlled the thrusting now, achingly slow and steady, mimicking my rhythm. I fumbled for the egg and moved it off center. The last thing I needed was to go over the edge too soon.

Because I wanted to float here forever, my whole being, my whole existence distilled into a burning ring of pleasure.

Suddenly Greg pulled out, leaving me empty again.

I cried out, almost sobbing with disappointment.

Before I could protest, he jammed the toy back inside my aching asshole. I heard the snap of a condom. He probed me again, lower, and slid deep into my cunt, bareback, the combination of dick and toy teasing my G-spot deliciously.

This was definitely new. Greg had always come in my ass before, but I liked this, too, being fucked in stereo. Greg began to pump harder. He was close. I embraced the butt plug like a long-lost lover and moved the egg directly to my clit.

Now all my secret places were stretched, burning, battered.

There was no feeling like it in the whole world.

When I came, my orgasm rolled up my torso, a twisted ball of fire and pain shattering my head open, pouring from my throat in a shriek of pleasure.

Greg slammed into me. I gripped him tightly as he came, too, with low, barking grunts. I fell forward and he collapsed on top, panting.

As always, our cool-down ritual was quicker: wrap the plug in Kleenex, mop up with the towel, fall into each other's arms, slick and sweaty, laughing like kids stumbling off the fastest, wildest roller coaster in the park.

"Jesus," I breathed, "that just gets better every time. The two-for-one fuck was great."

"Only the best for you, sweetie. Did you like your present?" he asked, stroking my hair.

"I loved it, the little sparkly fucker. How long was he waiting for me in there?"

"A couple of weeks. You've been too well behaved lately. Good thing you slipped up with your assignment today."

"That reminds me, I'm starving. Let me wash up and I'll go get you some fancy-ass pasta like a good girl."

I hadn't told him yet, but it always gave me a secret thrill to saunter through the aisles of our local gourmet market after a good butt-fucking.

"I'll come with you," Greg replied, giving me a squeeze. "I want to be sure you get just what we need."

I had to smile. That was one thing I could always count on.

YOUR HAND ON MY NECK

Rachel Kramer Bussel

for A.

Your hand on my neck is all it takes to make tears race to my eyes, to put my body on red alert, to let me know that I'm about to go insane. It's that simple...yet of course, your fingers going for the jugular will always be more complex than I can ever truly describe. It's the fastest way to get my attention, to snap me out of whatever place my mind has wandered, back to where it should be: on you. Forget about when you raise your hand to spank me or reach for my nipples to pinch them or even when you grab my arm to shackle my wrist to your bedposts, all of which you know I adore; your hand on my neck is what makes me unbearably, almost impossibly, wet.

Is it because you were my first? Is it because I trust you more? Or is it because those tears that rush forth, the gasps that claw their way to the surface, the panic that bubbles just below the surface, speak to me in a language deeper than words ever could?

Sometimes, because you know me so well, because you know what it does to me, you do it while we're sitting across from each other at a restaurant. To an outsider, it probably looks like a light caress, like your hand could just as easily be stroking my arm, your thumb caressing my inner wrist, or smoothing my hair, or tracing my lips. And you could be doing any of those things, but you're not: You're wrapping yourself from thumb to forefinger around the expanse of my neck, pressing just enough to make my lips go slack, my breath get short. You're telling me so much without saying a word, and my first instinct is to do what I do in bed: bend my head back, elongate my neck, shut my eyes, give more of myself to you.

But we're in public, so I wait, and soon the moment passes. A couple can hold hands, under or even above the table, or play footsie, with no problem, but the intimacy of choking is probably pushing the envelope, even in Manhattan. Still, I think about it, even while waiting for my burger and fries, about how it feels when you press harder, when my throat constricts and the gasps become sobs and I want to thrash and struggle so I can feel you clamp down harder.

That's what happens when we're at home, alone. We'll be making out, giggling, me lying next to you, rubbing the wiry, warm fur on your chest. One minute I'm kissing whatever part of your skin is closest, and the next you've flipped me over. Any clothes I might've been wearing disappear real fast. Your fingers are hard, strong, insistent, all ten finding my most vulnerable places and staking their claim. Actually, that may not be totally true. Five slam down against my neck, and I arch it and my back up to meet you, while other fingers slam hard inside me. Usually, I like to talk, but I have nothing to say now, even if I could make more than strangled noises.

I want many things at once, but I know you have only so

many hands, so many ways to torture me, so I have to wait and
see which of your methods you'll choose today. I've never told
you this, but no one else has ever made me want them to squeeze
me right there so powerfully. I won't lie: I've been choked before. I've had a hand over my mouth, had my head shoved into
a pillow, been muffled and gagged by other men. But no one has
ever made me want it like this. I wonder sometimes if there's
some secret button inside me, invisible to everyone but you, that
you know to press, to lean on, that makes me so wild, because
I swear that when you put your hand there, when your eyes go
from easy to a little angry, when your voice goes gruff and deep
and a little mean, when your hand becomes, for these sweet moments, the sexiest of weapons, I would do anything for you.

Maybe I don't have to tell you, maybe you can see it in my
eyes, because without my having to ask, you climb on top of me,
keeping your hand firm so all I can really move is the rest of me,
from my neck down, yet those parts don't matter as much. It's
all in my head, literally, all the blood and passion and lust and
masochism and need. That, plus my oral fixation, means that
when you wrap your legs on either side of my face and present
your cock to me, I open as wide as I possibly can. Your balls
hit my chin and your half-hard cock slides against my tongue,
and I shift what little I can to make my mouth as wet and tight
as possible for you. Your hand tightens on my neck while your
other one grabs the back of my head and lifts it up to meet you,
positions me where you need me to be.

There's really no other way to say what we're doing: you're
fucking my face, my mouth, slamming into me over and over.
You tilt my head so the tip presses against my cheek and I drool
and struggle to keep up. You briefly let up on my neck and I
breathe in deep, wish for a smack across the cheek, a hard, stinging one, but I don't get it. That's the kind of request I find hard

to make, because to ask for it is to admit to a level of perversity from which there's no return, though perhaps that's a silly distinction because here you are choking me with such precision, then molding my mouth to your cock. My pussy almost hurts, I'm so turned on, but I don't want you to fuck me, not with your dick, not now, because that would take away from what you're going to give me very soon: your come all over my face.

You know I want that, know I love when you beat your dick against me, shove your balls in my mouth, but you make me wait, perhaps because you know how bad I need it. You tease me, the insides of my mouth your personal sex toy as you rub the head there, denying me all of you all the way down. Your hand cups my neck while you rub your cock up and down my face, in my mouth, wherever you want. "Do you want my come, you little whore?" you ask as you jerk yourself off above me, your hand doing the job I should, rightfully, be doing. If my arms weren't bound above my head, I'd be reaching down and touching my clit, maybe slapping myself lightly there, pushing my fingers inside, anything for relief from the intensity that's overtaken me down there. Instead, I just press my legs tightly together, squeeze my inner muscles, try to inch closer before I feel that first hot drop hit me. I open wide and you slide inside, practically melting into me, your fingers seeking out my hard nipple and twisting it around as you explode. You manage to pull out before it's all gone, to moisturize me with a cream so rich Lancôme could never hope to compete.

I only think about it later, after we're done, when your come is drying on my skin, how much I loved you choking me, not being able to breathe in the usual way, only moving the parts of me you wanted me to.

Last week, you gave me a special gift: two hands there, each taking half, the pressure greater than one alone could handle.

Your dick got even harder as you slammed into me, your weight
shifting into your arms, making it hard for me to swallow. The
shallow sound of my breath was loud in my ears as I willed you
to twist a little. I longed for clothespins, imagined them standing upright on my nipples. You pulled one hand away to slap my
clit, and I turned my head to the side, beckoning to the sheet,
asking it for something I couldn't ask of you. You knew, though,
and tightening your grip on my neck, you slapped my cheek, the
sting ringing in my ear. Slapping my face requires much more
precision than spanking my ass. A stray slap down there can
be corrected easily; a misplaced stroke can stop everything up
above. Maybe because you've hit my sweet spot countless times,
you know where on my face I crave it most, that fleshy apple
bulge of my cheekbone, the part that makes me flinch, my teeth
clamped. I look up at you through filmy eyes; I can't look too
directly because that would be too much, for both of us. There
has to be a veil for me to let you do this. It's why you'd stroke
my neck across the table at a restaurant, or even lightly pinch
my cheek, but would never in a million years slap me like this.
Even a tap on the ass can be tolerated in public, but not this.
This is more depraved somehow, and we both know it. My lips
start to tremble, and you lift your hand from my neck to cover
them. You wind up covering part of my nose, too, and I force
the panic to wind its way back down my throat before you slap
my cheek again. Your dick is still inside me, but I wouldn't say
you're fucking me with it, more like holding me in place, making sure I know you could fuck me at any time.

You switch hands and smack my right cheek, and I make
sure my eyes are adamantly shut so I don't see the blows coming,
don't know what's going to happen, because that would ruin it a
little bit for me. I feel you pull out and fear it's over, fear you've
tired of me, are bored by what's increasingly becoming less of

a game and more of a need. But instead your hand lingers on my face, seeing how much of it you can cover. I arch up against you, my back curving, straining to be covered by you. You give me what I want, pinching my nose, just for a minute, but long enough to make my insides seize up. You let go but then your face is right next to mine, the stubble I adore so much brushing against my cheek. I think you're going to whisper something to me, but instead you bite me there, the fleshy part of my lower jaw. Not hard, but I'm sure it'll leave an imprint. My clit is aching, but I can't think about that too much because you grab my hands in yours and then tickle me under my arms. You're not supposed to do that; tickling is off limits, but you do it anyway, followed by a sharp slap across my face, first one, then the other cheek. I want to ask you to do it harder, but I just think it, wondering if you'd be insulted were I to make such a request.

You take my silence for disinterest and do, indeed, slap me harder. Maybe it's my imagination but you jab your cock into me when you do it. I've only slapped someone's face in real anger, not like this, so I don't know what it's like, but I hope it makes you hard, I hope hurting me gets you off the way lying beneath you does to me. I don't want to ask because as much as I may imagine what you're feeling, I'd prefer you to show me with your body rather than your words.

You pull out and then shove your fingers into me, hard, claiming me, before finding something better to do. You turn me over and shove my face into the pillow. I breathe into it as you hold me down. This is more impersonal than when you choke me, and I'm not sure which I like better. You can't slap my face or spit in it or see it like this, but you can make sure I know my breathing—or not—is up to you. You can let go and know I'll stay there, still, waiting for you to lift my head. You can attach the brand-new spreader bar, the one you told me about in great detail but have thus far withheld, to my ankles. I never used to think not moving my legs was such a big deal; my wrists, yes—they're as sensitive as my neck, and even the lightest of scarves gives me goose bumps. But like this, facedown, like I could be any girl, any body, my wetness right there for you to see, or stuff, or slap, I get it. I get what it means to let you have me on your terms.

I get that you know how good it's going to feel when you once again force your cock inside me, because I'm so tight. I get that it's not really about my neck at all, not even about my pussy. It's about not having a say, having to wait for every breath. It's about going to that place where nothing else matters except where you'll touch me next, if you'll touch me next. It's about going to a place where I have no control—of my movements, my thoughts, my tears. Those start to soak the pillow, and you lift my face to look at me, keeping me twisted there when I try to burrow back in. You don't rush to untie me, thankfully, but stroke my cheek with your thumb, then move it down, pressing into my neck, grabbing my nipple. You get up, and I sink back against the bed, before lifting myself up for the collar, the one that's a little wide, that you buckle almost, but not quite, too tight.

Then something new is inside me, something piercing, cold, hard. Metal, I think. I shudder at the weight of it, and the realization that you want to come in my mouth, that this is just a way to butter me up, to make me frantic before I get filled up. You massage the entrance to my sex, the sleek lips that are now swollen and tender, working the toy deeper inside. In truth, I don't know if I like it, because you're teasing me with it, edging it just far enough but not letting me wiggle back against it. I get used to this flirtation, and just when I do, you shove it all the way inside me. I feel like I have to pee, and twist from side to side. "Take it," you say, your voice deep, hard, unyielding.

I do, at first, for you, because I don't want to fail here. Then I take it for me, for the precipice of pleasure you make me teeter on. I take it for all the reasons I'm scared, for all the ways this shakes me to my core. I take it because I like the tears, like the pain; take it because, for whatever twisted, crazy reasons, my body responds. My pussy and brain stop battling and simply agree to let you go there, go to that place that seems almost impossible to take, yet like some drawn-out video game, the reward is yet to come. Your hand goes tight around my neck, you must be leaning your weight there, even as the metal drills into me. Your spit lands on my face, first next to my lips, then on them. You lean down and bite me, not my neck or my nipple, but my breast, a place you say with your teeth is more for you than me.

Yet somehow, every inch of my body, because it's yours, responds to you. Each breath that tries to escape and doesn't boomerangs back in arousal, doubling, tripling, multiplying my excitement to infinity. Part of me doesn't want to come, just wants to see how much fuel you can add to my fire, how much you can make me want the pain, the torment. I flash on an image of you dragging me down into the hotel pool, then pulling me up but covering my lips with yours. I think of the many ways you've tested me. You tell me to open my eyes and even though I don't really want to, I do. I'm afraid of what I'll see, because it's much easier to face the ways our kinks intertwine when I don't have to do so literally. Seeing your hand coming toward my face, after you've placed my hand on the toy and insisted I slam it deep, is more intense than the ensuing slap could ever be. You've told me you want to set up a mirror so I can watch you strangle me, watch myself almost go limp, and I've resisted.

The toy is no longer so cold, and I know I'm on the verge.

You take it out and soon replace it with something even bigger, something my body responds to by clenching shut. "I can't," I say softly, sure that it's true, but you let up on me and take the time to slather me with lube.

"You can and you will," you say, and I try to relax as best I can, even though every instinct in me is telling me what you're attempting is impossible. I can take your hands wrapped around my throat, crave it even, but this toy is twice the size of your cock, or feels that way, anyway. You've told me before that you think about a man with a giant dick fucking me while you hold me down, pinning me there, forcing me to shut up if I scream by making me suck you. I think about that as the toy slowly sinks inside. It gets about halfway, which already feels bigger than having a fist inside me. I take slow, measured breaths, a sign of my freedom, before your hand clamps down, twisting my head sideways, covering my nose, like you don't want to look at me. I know you do, you just want to see me raw, messy, tear-streaked and sweaty, my face covered in come. You want to see me helpless without you.

I turn over at your command and press my head into the sheets, smell the detergent more than the sex in the air. You spank me while you hold the dildo there, pushing it in when I try to squeeze it out. I don't cry, not out loud, anyway. I don't think about coming even when I do, even when I gush. I think about you, about how you look at me before, during and after. I think about how you take me to the brink, and sometimes I don't want to come back. I think about you tightening the collar as far as it will go. I think about how lucky I am that we aren't doing any of this for each other, at least, not *just* for each other, but for ourselves. I'd hate being the recipient of a pity choke, a mercy slap, a charity face-fuck.

You don't hold me gently when we're done, at least, not yet.

Later, when we sleep, you'll be greedy, grabbing my leg to drape it over you, my arm to stick to yours. Now, you push me onto my back again and put your hand there. I'm sore and tired and spent; wasted, really, but still, that's once again all it takes, your hand on my neck, like it belongs there.

ABOUT THE AUTHORS

HEIDI CHAMPA's work appears in more than ten anthologies including *Tasting Him, Frenzy* and *Girl Fun One,* as well as in *Bust* magazine, and in electronic form, Clean Sheets, Ravenous Romance, Oysters and Chocolate, and the Erotic Woman. Find her online at heidichampa.blogspot.com.

ELIZABETH COLDWELL's short stories have appeared in several anthologies with a BDSM flavor, including *Yes, Sir; Spanked* and *Bottoms Up.*

Based on her own explorations in the world of D/s and BDSM, **TESS DANESI** explores the darker side of erotica, writing with raw honesty about that shadowy area where pain becomes pleasure and pleasure, pain. She blogs at Urban Gypsy (nyc-urban-gypsy.blogspot.com) and has been published in several anthologies and *Time Out New York.*

JUSTINE ELYOT has contributed short stories to a number of erotica anthologies and recently published her first full-length book, *On Demand*. She lives in the United Kingdom.

EMERALD's erotic fiction has been published in anthologies such as *Swing!* edited by Jolie duPre, *Love Notes* and *Tasting Her* edited by Rachel Kramer Bussel, *K Is for Kinky* edited by Alison Tyler, and *Best Women's Erotica 2006* edited by Violet Blue. Visit her online at thegreenlightdistrict.org.

SHANNA GERMAIN's writings have appeared in places like *Absinthe Literary Review, Best American Erotica, Best Gay Bondage, Best Gay Erotica, Best Gay Romance, Best Lesbian Erotica, Best Lesbian Romance, Dirty Girls, X: The Erotic Treasury, Yes, Sir* and more. Visit her online at shannagermain.com.

ARIEL GRAHAM lives and writes in Northern Nevada with her husband and way, way too many cats. Her work can be found in *Call of the Dark, Frenzy, Never Have the Same Sex Twice* and *Best Lesbian Romance 2009*.

ISABELLE GRAY's writing appears in many anthologies.

DOUG HARRISON's short stories appear in twenty anthologies. His spiritual memoir, *In Pursuit of Ecstasy*, is online. He was active in San Francisco's gay and pansexual leather scenes. Doug appears in nine erotic videos and also professional photo shoots. He was Mr. June for the San Francisco AIDS Emergency Fund *1999 Bare Chest Calendar*.

MERCY LOOMIS graduated from college one class short of an accidental certificate in folklore. She has a BA in psychology, but don't hold that against her. Her favorite pastimes include practicing Urban Krav Maga, playing *Rock Band*, and studying ancient history. She and her husband live near Madison, Wisconsin.

Prolific author of hundreds of dirty tales and ringleader of the Blow Hard Tour 2009, **SOMMER MARSDEN's** anthology *Lucky 13* was released in April 2009. Sommer lives in Maryland where you might spot her drinking red wine or running but not simultaneously. Visit her openly naughty world at SmutGirl. blogspot.com.

EVAN MORA is a recovering corporate banker who's thrilled to put pen to paper after years of daydreaming in boardrooms. Her work can be found in *Best Lesbian Erotica 2009, Best Lesbian Romance '09* and *'10, Where the Girls Are* and *The Sweetest Kiss: Ravishing Vampire Erotica.*

AIMEE PEARL is the nom de plume of a kinky bisexual submissive living in that perverted paradise known as San Francisco. Her erotic adventures appear in *Best Women's Erotica, Best Lesbian Erotica* and *On Our Backs* magazine, among other places. In this volume's story, written for Sir, every word is true.

REMITTANCE GIRL lives in exile in Vietnam, where she writes, designs multimedia and grows orchids. Her work has appeared in a number of erotic anthologies, including *The Sweetest Kiss* and *Girls on Top.* Her website is at remittancegirl.com.

LISABET SARAI has published five erotic novels, including her new paranormal *Serpent's Kiss* and her thriller *Exposure,* and two short-story collections. She also reviews erotica for Erotica

Readers and Writers Association, and Erotica Revealed. Visit Lisabet online at Lisabet's Fantasy Factory (lisabetsarai.com).

KISSA STARLING (kissastarling.com) began writing in a diary as a young girl. In school she passed notes and penned short poems to pass around the classroom. She finds inspiration in everything around her: the changing of the seasons, sunsets, rides on the back of a Harley and romantic evenings with her husband.

CHARLOTTE STEIN has had seven short stories published in various Black Lace anthologies, including *Lust at First Bite* and *Sexy Little Numbers: Best Women's Erotica from Black Lace*. Her collection of short stories, *The Things That Make Me Give In*, was published in October 2009.

DONNA GEORGE STOREY is the author of *Amorous Woman* (Neon/Orion), a semiautobiographical tale of an American's steamy love affair with Japan. Her short fiction has appeared in numerous anthologies including *Best American Erotica*, *He's on Top*, *Peep Show*, *Spanked* and *Bottoms Up*. Read more of her work at DonnaGeorgeStorey.com.

ALISON TYLER has penned twenty-five naughty novels, edited fifty erotic anthologies, and written more than one thousand dirty stories. Her most recent anthology is *Pleasure Bound* (Cleis Press, 2009). Find her 24/7 at alisontyler.blogspot.com.

YOLANDA WEST is fifty-three years old and lives in the Cleveland area. She works for a government agency by day and writes naughty stories by night. She is married with two grown sons. One of her stories appeared in *The MILF Anthology*.

SALOME WILDE is the unsubtle pen name of an academic who relishes writing creatively and living fully. Her erotica has been published in such print anthologies as *Best American Erotica 2006, X: An Erotic Treasury* and *Sex and Candy* as well as magazines and online publications.

ABOUT
THE EDITOR

RACHEL KRAMER BUSSEL (rachelkramerbussel.com) is a New York–based author, editor and blogger. She is the *Best Sex Writing* series editor (bestsexwriting.com), and has edited or coedited more than twenty books of erotica, including *Peep Show; Bottoms Up: Spanking Good Stories; Spanked; Naughty Spanking Stories from A to Z 1* and *2; The Mile High Club; Do Not Disturb; Tasting Him; Tasting Her; Yes, Sir; Yes, Ma'am; He's on Top; She's on Top; Caught Looking; Hide and Seek; Crossdressing; Rubber Sex; Sex and Candy; Ultimate Undies; Glamour Girls; Bedding Down* and *Please, Ma'am*. Her work has been published in more than one hundred anthologies, including *Best American Erotica 2004* and *2006*, Zane's *Chocolate Flava 2* and *Purple Panties, Everything You Know About Sex Is Wrong, Single State of the Union* and *Desire: Women Write About Wanting*. She serves as senior editor at *Penthouse Variations*, and wrote the popular "Lusty Lady" column for the *Village Voice*.

Rachel has written for *AVN, Bust,* Cleansheets.com, *Cosmopolitan, Curve,* The Daily Beast Fresh Yarn, TheFrisky.com, Gothamist, Huffington Post, Mediabistro, *Newsday, New York Post, Penthouse, Playgirl, Radar, San Francisco Chronicle, Tango, Time Out New York* and *Zink,* among others. She has appeared on "The Martha Stewart Show," "The Berman and Berman Show," NY1, and Showtime's "Family Business." She has hosted In the Flesh Erotic Reading Series (inthefleshreadingseries.com) since October 2005, which has featured everyone from Susie Bright to Zane, and about which the *New York Times*'s UrbanEye newsletter said she "welcomes eroticism of all stripes, spots and textures." Read more about *Please, Sir* at http://pleasesirbook.wordpress.com.